The Borrowers Aloft

by
Mary Norton

Illustrated by Diana Stanley

London
J. M. Dent & Sons Limited

Mary Norton spent ~~much of her childhood in a~~ large Georgian house which later became the model for Firbank Hall in 'The Borrowers'. She was educated at convent schools and spent a happy year as an actress at the Old Vic before she married and went to live in Portugal—her husband's family being ship-owners domiciled in Portugal for several generations.

During the war she was evacuated to New York and struggled to support herself and her four children while her husband was in the Navy. It was at this time that Mary Norton began writing in earnest—short stories, articles, translations—but it was not until later that she wrote down some of the stories she told her children.

On her return to England she went back to the stage for a while, but a new career was beginning and in 1945 her first children's book 'The Magic Bed-Knob' was published, followed by 'Bonfires and Broomsticks'. These two stories were later published as one revised volume—'Bed-Knob and Broomstick', which has now been made into a feature film. Then came the 'Borrowers' books—four delightful and original stories of people of Lilliputian size: 'The Borrowers' (awarded the Carnegie Medal, 1952), 'The Borrowers Afield', 'The Borrowers Afloat', 'The Borrowers Aloft'—and the short story 'Poor Stainless'.

Since 1972 Mary Norton has lived in County Cork with her second husband, in a Queen Anne house which they have renovated beautifully, and it was here that her latest book was written—'Are All the Giants Dead?'—a completely new and fascinating story of a modern boy involved with fairy-tale characters.

© Text, Mary Norton, 1961
© Illustrations, J. M. Dent & Sons Ltd, 1961
First published in this edition 1975

ISBN 0 460 05107 5

THIS STORY IS DEDICATED WITH LOVE TO
TOM BRUNSDON AND FRANCES RUSH
AND TO ALL THE CHILDREN IN THE WORLD
WHO HAVE PROMISED THEIR PARENTS NEVER TO
PLAY WITH GAS, AND WHO KEEP THEIR PROMISES

CHAPTER ONE

SOME PEOPLE thought it strange that there should be two model villages, one so close to the other (there was a third as a matter of fact belonging to a little girl called Agnes Mercy Foster, which nobody visited, and which we need not bother about because it was not built to last).

One model village was at Fordham, called Little Fordham: it belonged to Mr Pott. Another was at Went-le-Craye, called Ballyhoggin, and belonged to Mr Platter.

It was Mr Pott who started it all, quietly and happily for his own amusement; and it was the business-like Mr Platter, for quite another reason, who copied Mr Pott.

Mr Pott was a railway-man who had lost his leg on the railway: he lost it at dusk one evening on a lonely stretch of line—not through carelessness, but when saving the life of a badger. Mr Pott had always been anxious about these creatures: the single track ran through a wood, and in the half light the badgers would trundle out, sniffing their way across the sleepers. Only at certain times of the year were they in any real danger, and that was when the early dusk (the time they liked to sally forth) coincided with the passing of the last train from Hatter's Cross. After the train passed the night would be quiet again; and foxes, hares and rabbits could cross the line with safety; and nightingales would sing in the wood.

In those early days of the railway, Mr Pott's small, lonely signal-box was almost a home from home. He had there his kettle, his oil-lamps, his plush-covered table and his broken-springed railway armchair. To while away the long hours between trains, he had his fret-saw, his stamp collection and a well-thumbed copy of the Bible which sometimes he would read aloud. Mr Pott was a good man, very kind and gentle. He loved his fellow creatures almost as much as he loved his trains. With the fret-saw he would make collecting-boxes for the Railway Benevolent Fund; these were

shaped like little houses and he made them from old cigar-boxes, and no two of his houses were alike. On the first Sunday of every month Mr Pott, on his bicycle, would make a tour of the village, armed with a screwdriver and a small black bag. At each home or hostelry he would unscrew the roof of a little house and count out the contents into his bag. Sometimes he was cheated (but not often) and would mutter sadly as he rode away: 'Fox been at the eggs again.'

Occasionally, in his signal-box, Mr Pott would paint a picture, very small and detailed. He had painted two of the church, three of the vicarage, two of the post office, three of the forge and one of his own signal-box. These pictures he would give away as prizes to those who collected most for his fund.

On the night of which we speak the badger bit Mr Pott—that was the trouble. It made him lose his balance, and in that moment's delay the train wheels caught his foot. Mr Pott never saw the marks of the badger's teeth because the leg it bit was the leg they cut off. The badger itself escaped unharmed.

The Railway Benevolent were very generous. They gave Mr Pott a small lump sum and found him a cottage just outside the village, where three tall poplar-trees stood beside a stream. It was here, on a mound in his garden, that he started to build his railway.

First he bought at second hand a set of model trains. He saw them advertised in a local paper with the electric battery on which to run them. Because there was no room large enough in his tiny cottage he set up the lines in his garden. With the help of the blacksmith he made the rails but he needed no help with the sleepers: these he cut to scale and set them firmly, as of old he had set the big ones. Once these were set he tarred them over, and when the sun was hot they smelled just right. Mr Pott would sit on the hard ground, his wooden leg stretched out before him, and close his eyes and sniff the railway smell. Lovely it was, and magic—but something was missing. Smoke, that's what it was! Yes, he badly needed some smoke—not only the tang of it, but the sight of it as well. Later, with the help of Miss Menzies of High Beech, he found a solution.

When he made his signal-box, he built it of solid brick. It was exactly like his old one, wooden stairs and all. He glazed the windows with real glass and made them to open and shut (it wasn't for nothing, he realized then, that he had kept the hinges of all the cigar-boxes passed on to him by his directors). The bricks he made from the red brick of his tumbledown pigsty; he pounded these down to a fine dust and mixed them loosely with cement. He set the mixture

in a criss-cross mould which he stood on a large tin tea-tray. The mould was made of old steel corset-bones—a grill of tiny rectangles soldered by the blacksmith. With his contraption, Mr Pott could make five hundred bricks at a time. Sometimes to vary the colour he stirred in powdered ochre or a drop of cochineal. He slated the roof of his signal-box with thin flakes of actual slate, neatly trimmed to scale—these too from his ruined pigsty.

Before he put the roof on he took a lump of builder's putty. Rolling and rubbing it between his stiff old hands, he made four small sausages for arms and legs and a thicker,

shorter one for the body. Rolling and squeezing, he
egg for the head and smoothed it squarely on to the shoulders. Then he pinched it here and there and carved bits out,
scraping away with a horny thumb-nail.

But it wasn't very good, even as an effigy—let alone as a
self-portrait. To make it more like himself he took off the
leg at the knee and stuck in a match-stick. Then when the

putty was hardened he painted the figure over with a decent
suit of railway blue, pinked up the face, gummed on a thatch
of greying hair made from that creeper called old-man's-
beard, and set it up in his signal-box. There it looked much
more human—and really rather frightening, standing so still
and stiff and staring through the windows.

The signal-box seemed real enough though—with its outside stairway of seasoned wood, yellow lichen on the slates,
weathered bricks with their softly blended colours, windows
ajar and, every now and again, the living clack of its signals.

The children of the village became rather a nuisance. They

would knock on his front door and ask to see the railway. Mr Pott, once settled comfortably on the hard ground, his wooden leg stuck out before him, found it hard to rise quickly. But, being very patient, he would heave himself up and stump along to let in his callers. He would greet them civilly and conduct them down the passage, through the scullery and out into the garden. There precious building time was lost in questions, answers and general exclamation. Sometimes while they talked his cement would dry, or his soldering-iron grow cold. After a time he made the rule that they could only come at week-ends, and on Saturdays and Sundays he would leave his door ajar. On the scullery table he set a small collecting-box and the grown-ups, who now came too, were asked to pay one penny: the proceeds he sent to his Fund. The children still came free.

After he made his station, more and more people were interested and the proceeds began to mount up. The station was an exact copy of Fordham's own station, and he called it Little Fordham. The letters were picked out in white stone on a bank of growing moss. He furnished the inside before he put the roof on. In the waiting-rooms, hard dark benches, and in the station-master's office, pigeon-holes for tickets and a high wooden desk. The blacksmith (a young man called Henry who by now was deeply interested) welded him a fireplace of dark wrought iron. They burned dead moss and pine-needles to test the draught and they saw that the chimney drew.

But once the roof was on all these details were lost. There was no way to see inside except by lying down and peering through the windows, and when the platform was completed you couldn't do even this. The platform roof was edged by Mr Pott with a wooden fringe of delicate fretwork.

There were cattle-pens, milk-churns; and old-fashioned station lamps in which Mr Pott could burn oil.

With Mr Pott's meticulous attention to detail and refusal to compromise with second best, the building of the station took two years and seven months. And then he started on his village.

CHAPTER TWO

MR POTT had never heard of Mr Platter, nor Mr Platter of Mr Pott.

Mr Platter was a builder and undertaker at Went-le-Craye, the other side of the river, of which Mr Pott's stream was a tributary. They lived quite close, as the crow flies, but far apart by road. Mr Platter had a fine, new red brick house on the main road to Bedford, with a gravel drive, and a garden which sloped to the water. He had built it himself and called it Ballyhoggin. Mr Platter had amassed a good deal of money. But people weren't dying as they used to; and when the brick factory closed down there were fewer new inhabitants. This was because Mr Platter, building gimcrack villas for the workers, had spoiled the look of the countryside.

Some of Mr Platter's villas were left on his hands, and he would advertise them in county papers as 'suitable for elderly retired couples'. He was annoyed if, in desperation, he had to let to a bride and bridegroom: because Mr Platter was very good at arranging expensive funerals and he liked to stock-up on an older type of client. He had a tight kind of face and a pair of rimless glasses which caught the light so that you could not see his eyes. He had, however, a very polite and gentle manner; so you took the eyes on trust. Dear Mr Platter, the mourners said, was always 'so very kind', and they seldom questioned his bill.

Mr Platter was small and thin but Mrs Platter was large. Both had rather mauvish faces: Mr Platter's had a violet tinge while Mrs Platter's inclined more to pink. Mrs Platter was an excellent wife and both of them worked very hard.

As villas fell vacant and funerals became scarcer, Mr Platter had time on his hands. He had never liked spare time. In order to get rid of it he took up gardening. All Mr Platter's flowers were kept like captives—firmly tied to stakes: the slightest sway or wriggle was swiftly punished— a lop here or a cut there. Very soon the plants gave in— uncomplaining as guardsmen they would stand to attention in rows. His lawns too were a sight to behold as, weed-repelled and mown in stripes, they sloped down to the river. A glimpse of Mr Platter with his weeding-tools was enough to make the slyest dandelion seed smartly change course in mid air, and it was said of a daisy plant that, realizing suddenly where it was, the pink-fringed petals turned white overnight.

Mrs Platter, for her part—and with an eye to the main road and its traffic—put up a notice which said TEAS, and she set up a stall on the grass verge for the sale of flowers and fruit. They did not do very well, however, until Mrs Platter had an inspiration and changed the wording of the notice to RIVERSIDE TEAS. Then people did stop. And once conducted to the tables behind the house they would have the 'set tea' because there was no other. This was expensive, although there was margarine instead of butter and falsely pink, oozy jam bought by Mrs Platter straight from the factory in large tin containers. She also sold soft drinks in glass bottles with marble stoppers, toy balloons and paper windmills. People kept coming and the Platters began to do well; the cyclists were glad to sit down for a while, and the motorists to take off their dust-coats and goggles and stretch their legs.

The falling-off was gradual. At first they hardly noticed it. 'Quiet Whitsun,' Mr Platter would say as they changed the position of the tables so as not to damage the lawn. He thought again about an ice-cream machine, but decided to wait: Mr Platter was a great believer in what he described as 'laying out money', but only where he saw a safe return.

Instead of this he mended up his old flat-bottomed boat and, with the aid of a shrimping-net, he cleared the stream of scum. 'Boating' he wanted to add to the tea-notice; but Mrs Platter dissuaded him. There might be complaints, she thought, as with the best will in the world and a bit of pulling and pushing, you could get the boat round the nettle-infested island but that would be about all.

August Bank Holiday was a fiasco: only ten set teas sold on what Mrs Platter called 'The Saturday'; eleven on the Sunday and seven on the Monday. 'I can't make it out,' Mrs Platter kept saying, as she and Agnes Mercy threw the stale loaves into buckets for the chickens. 'Last year they were standing for tables. . . .'

Agnes Mercy was fifteen now. She had grown into a large, slow, watchful girl, who seemed older than her age. This

was her first job—called 'helping Mrs Platter with the teas'.

'Mrs Read's doing teas too now,' said Agnes Mercy one day, when they were cutting bread and butter.

'Mrs Read of Fordham? Mrs Read of the Crown and Anchor?' Mrs Platter seldom went to Fordham—it was what she called 'out of her way'.

'That's right,' said Agnes Mercy.

'Teas in the garden?'

Agnes Mercy nodded. 'And in the orchard. Next year they're converting the barn.'

'But what does she give them? I mean, she hasn't got a river. Does she give them strawberries?'

Agnes Mercy shook her head. 'No,' she said, 'it's because of the model railway . . .' and in her slow way, under a fire of questions, she told Mrs Platter about Mr Pott.

'A model railway . . .' remarked Mrs Platter thoughtfully, after a short reflective silence. 'Well, two can play at that game!'

Mr Platter whipped up a model railway in no time at all. There was not a moment to lose: and he laid out money in a big way. Mr Pott was a slow worker but he was several years ahead. All Mr Platter's builders were called in. A bridge was built to the island; the island was cleared of weeds; paths and turf were laid down; electric batteries installed. Mr Platter went up to London and bought two sets of the most expensive trains on the market, goods and passengers. He bought two railway stations, both exactly alike, but far more modern than the railway station at Little Fordham. Experts came down from London to install his signal-boxes and to adjust his lines and points. It was all done in less than three months.

And it worked. By the very next summer to RIVERSIDE TEAS they added the words MODEL RAILWAY.

And the people poured in.

Mr Platter had to clear a field and face it with rubble for parking the motor-cars. In addition to the set teas, it cost a shilling to cross the bridge and visit the railway. Half way through the summer the paths on the island became worn down and he refaced them with asphalt, and built a second bridge to keep people moving. And he put the price up to one and sixpence.

There was soon an asphalted car park and a special field for wagonettes, and a stone trough with running water for the horses. Parties would often picnic in this field, leaving it strewn with litter.

But none of this bothered Mr Pott. He was not particularly anxious for visitors: they took up his time and disturbed his work. If he encouraged sightseers at all it was just out of loyalty to his beloved Railway Benevolent.

He took no precautions for their comfort. It was Mrs Read of the Crown and Anchor saw to that side of things, and who benefited accordingly. The whole of Mr Pott's railway could be seen from the backdoor step which led on to his garden and sightseers had to pass through his house— they were welcome, of course, as they went through the kitchen, to a glass of cool water from the tap.

When Mr Pott built his church it was an exact copy of the Norman church at Fordham, with added steeple, grave-stones and all. He collected stone for over a year before he started to build. The stone-breakers helped him, as they

chipped beside the highway. So did Mr Flood, the mason. By now Mr Pott had several helpers in the village: besides Henry, the blacksmith, he had Miss Menzies of High Beech. Miss Menzies was very useful to Mr Pott, she designed Christmas cards for a living, wrote children's books and her hobbies were wood-carving, hand-weaving and barbola waxwork. She also believed in fairies.

When Mr Platter heard of the church—it took some time, because until it was finished, during visiting hours, Mr Pott swathed it in sacking—Mr Platter put up a larger one with a much higher steeple, based on Salisbury Cathedral. At a touch the windows lit up, and with the aid of a phonograph he laid on music inside. Takings had once more fallen off slightly at Ballyhoggin, now they leapt up again.

All the same, Mr Pott was a great worry to Mr Platter—you never quite knew what he might be up to, in his gentle plodding way. When Mr Pott built two cob cottages and thatched them, Mr Platter's takings fell off for weeks. Mr Platter was forced to screen off part of his island and build, at lightning speed, a row of semi-detached villas and a public house. The same thing happened when Mr Pott built his village shop and filled the window with miniature merchandise in painted barbola work—a gift from Miss Menzies of High Beech. Immediately, of course, Mr Platter built a row of shops and a hairdresser's establishment with a striped pole.

After a while, Mr Platter found a way of spying on Mr Pott.

CHAPTER THREE

HE MENDED up the flat-bottomed boat, which, for lack of use, had again become waterlogged.

Between the two villages, the weed-clogged river and its twisting, deep-cleft tributaries formed an irritating network, only to be circumvented by roads to distant bridges or by clambering and wading on foot. But if, thought Mr Platter, you could force a boat through the rushes you had a short cut and could spy on Mr Pott's house through the willows by his stream.

And this he did—after business hours on summer evenings. He did not like these expeditions but felt them to be his duty. Plagued by gnats, stung by horse-flies, scratched by brambles, when he arrived back to report to Mrs Platter he was always in a very bad temper. Sometimes he got stuck in the mud and sometimes, when the river was low, he had to clamber out into slime and frog-spawn to lift the boat over hidden obstructions such as drowned logs or barbed wire. But he found a place, a little past the poplars, where, standing on the stump of a willow, he could see the whole layout of Mr Pott's model village, and be screened himself by the flicker of silvery leaves.

'You shouldn't do it, love,' Mrs Platter would say when, panting, puce and perspiring, he sank on a bench in the garden. 'Not at your age and with your blood pressure.' But she had to agree, as she dabbed his gnat bites with ammonia or his wasp stings with dolly-blue, that taking it by and large his information was priceless. It was only due to Mr Platter's courage and endurance that they found out

16

about the model station-master and about Mr Pott's two
porters and the vicar in his cassock who stood at Mr Pott's
church door. Each of these tiny figures had been modelled
by Miss Menzies and dressed by her in suitable clothes which
she oiled to withstand the rain.

This discovery had shaken Mr Platter. It was just before

the opening of the season. 'Lifelike . . .' he kept saying,
'that's how you'd describe 'em. Madame Tussaud's isn't
in it. Why any one of 'em might *speak* to you, if you see what
I mean. It's enough to ruin you,' he concluded, 'and would
have if I hadn't seen 'em in time.'

However, he *had* seen them in time; and soon both the
model villages were inhabited. But Mr Platter's figures
seemed far less real than Mr Pott's. They were hurriedly
modelled, ready dressed in plaster of Paris and brightly

varnished over. To make up for this they were far more
varied and there were many more of them—postmen, milk-
men, soldiers, sailors and boy scouts. On the steps of his
church he put a bishop, surrounded by choir-boys, each of
the choir-boys looked like the others, each had a hymn-book
and a white plaster cassock; all had wide-open mouths.

'Now they are what I *would* call lifelike . . .' Mrs Platter
used to say proudly. And the organ would boom in the
church.

Then came the awful evening, long to be remembered,
when Mr Platter, returning from a boat trip, almost
stumbled as he climbed back on to the lawn. Mrs Platter,
at one of the tables, her large white cat on her lap, was peace-
fully counting out the takings; the littered garden was
bathed in evening sunlight, and the sleepy birds sang in the
trees.

'Whatever's the matter?' exclaimed Mrs Platter when she
saw Mr Platter's face.

He sank down heavily in the green chair opposite, shaking
the table and dislodging a pile of half-crowns. The cat,
alarmed and filled with foreboding, streaked off towards the
shrubbery. Mr Platter stared dully at the half-crowns as they
rolled away across the greensward but he did not stoop to
pick them up. Neither did Mrs Platter; she was staring at
Mr Platter's complexion: it looked most peculiar—a kind of
greenish heliotrope, very delicate in shade.

'Whatever's the matter? Go on, tell me! What's he been
and done now?'

Mr Platter looked back at her without any expression.
'We're done for,' he said.

'Nonsense. What he can do, we can do. And it's always

been like that. Remember the smoke. Now come on, tell
me!'

'Smoke,' exclaimed Mr Platter bitterly, 'that was nothing
—a bit of charred string! We soon got the hang of the
smoke. No, this is different; this is the end. We're finished,'
he added wearily.

'Why do you say that?'

Mr Platter got up from his chair and mechanically, as if

he did not know what he was doing, he picked up the fallen
half-crowns. He piled them up neatly, and pushed the pile
towards her. 'Got to look after the money now,' he said in
the same dull expressionless voice, and he slumped again in
his chair.

'Now, Sidney,' said Mrs Platter, 'this isn't like you—
you've got to show fight.'

'No good fighting', said Mr Platter, 'where the odds are
impossible. What he's done now is plain straightforward
impossible.'

His eyes strayed to the island where, touched with golden

light among the long evening shadows, the static plaster figures glowed dully, frozen in their attitudes—some seeming to run, some seeming to walk, some about to knock on doors and others simply sitting. Several windows of the model village glowed with molten sunlight as if they were afire. The birds hopped about amongst the houses, seeking for crumbs dropped by the visitors. Except for the birds, nothing moved . . . stillness and deadness.

Mr Platter blinked. 'And I'd set my heart on a cricket pitch,' he said huskily, 'bowler and batsmen and all.'

'Well, we still *can* have,' said Mrs Platter.

He looked at her pityingly. 'Not if they don't *play* cricket —don't you understand? I'm *telling* you—what he's done now is plain, straightforward impossible.'

'What has he done then?' asked Mrs Platter in a frightened voice, infected at last by the cat's foreboding.

Mr Platter looked back at her with haggard eyes. 'He's got a lot of live ones,' he said slowly.

CHAPTER FOUR

BUT MISS MENZIES—who believed in fairies, had seen them first. And in her girlish, excited, breathless way she had run to Mr Pott.

Mr Pott, busy with an inn-sign for his miniature Crown and Anchor, had said 'Yes' and 'No' and 'Really'. Sometimes hearing her voice rise to fever pitch, he would exclaim 'Get away' or 'You don't mean it'. The former expression had rather worried Miss Menzies at first. In a puzzled way her voice would falter and her blue eyes fill with tears. But soon she learned to value this request as the ultimate expression of Mr Pott's surprise: when Mr Pott said 'Get away' she took it as a compliment and would hug her knees and laugh.

'But it's *true*!' she would protest, shaking her head. 'They're alive! They're as much alive—as you and I are, and they've moved into Vine Cottage. . . . Why, you can see for yourself if you'd only look where they've even worn a path to the door!'

And Mr Pott, pincers in hand and inn-sign dangling, would glance down the slope towards his model of Vine Cottage. He would stare at the model for just long enough to please her and then, wondering what she was talking about, he would grunt a little and return to his work. 'Well, I never did,' he would say.

Mr Pott, once she 'got started', as he put it, never dreamed of listening to Miss Menzies. Though nodding and smiling, he would make his mind a blank. It was a trick which he had learned with his late wife, who was also known as a 'talker'. And Miss Menzies spoke in such a high, strange,

fanciful voice—using the oddest words and most fly-away
expressions; sometimes, to his dismay, she would even
recite poetry. He did not dislike her, far from it; he liked to
have her about, because in her strange, leggy, loping way
she always seemed girlishly happy, and her prattle, like
canary song, kept him cheerful. And many a debt he owed to
those restless fingers—concocting this and fashioning that:

not only could they draw, paint, sew, model and wood-carve, but they could slide into places where Mr Pott's own fingers, stiffer and stubbier, got stuck or could not reach. Quick as a flash, she was; gay as a lark and steady as a rock. '. . . none of us perfect,' he'd tell himself, 'you got to have something . . .' and with her it was 'talking'.

He knew she was not young, but when she sat beside him on the rough grass, clasping her thin wrists about her bent knees, swaying back and forth, her closed eyes raised to the sun and chattering nineteen to the dozen, she seemed to Mr Pott like some kind of overgrown schoolgirl. And sweet eyes she had too, when they were open—that he would say —for such a long, bony face: shy eyes, which slid away when you looked too long at them—more like violets, he'd say her eyes were, than forget-me-nots. They were shining now and so were the knuckles of her long fingers clasped too tightly about her knees; even her mouse-grey silky hair had a sudden lustre.

'The great secret, you see, is never to show that you've seen them. Stillness, stillness, that's the thing—and looking obliquely and never directly. Like with bird-watching . . .'

'. . . bird watching,' agreed Mr Pott, as Miss Menzies seemed to pause. Sometimes, to show his sympathy and disguise his lack of attention, Mr Pott would repeat the last word of Miss Menzies's last sentence; or sometimes anticipate Miss Menzies's last syllable. If Miss Menzies said: 'King and Coun——', Mr Pott would chip in, in an understanding voice, with '. . . tree'. Sometimes, being far away in mind, Mr Pott would make a mistake and Miss Menzies, referring to 'garden-produce', would find herself presented with '. . . roller' instead, and there would be bewilderment all round.

'I can't quite really, you know, make out quite *what* they are. I mean, from the size and that, you'd say they were fairies. Now, wouldn't you?' she challenged him.

'That's right,' said Mr Pott, testing the swing of his inn-sign with a stubby finger and wondering where he had left the oil.

'But you'd be wrong, you know. This little man I saw with this sack thing on his back—he was panting. Quite out of breath, he was. Now, fairies don't pant.' As Mr Pott was silent, Miss Menzies added sharply: 'Or do they?'

'Do they what?' asked Mr Pott, watching the swing of his inn-sign and wishing it did not squeak.

'Pant!' said Miss Menzies, and waited.

Mr Pott looked troubled. What could she be talking about? 'Pant?' he repeated. Mentally, he put the word into the plural, and with a glance at her face, took it out again. 'I wouldn't like to say,' he conceded cagily.

'Nor would I,' agreed Miss Menzies gaily, much to his relief. 'I mean—by and large—we know so little about fairies . . .'

'That's right,' said Mr Pott. He felt safe again.

'. . . what their habits are. I mean, whether or not they get tired or old like we do and go to bed, cook and do the housework. Or what they do about food. There's so little data. We don't even know what they . . .'

'. . . eat,' said Mr Pott.

'. . . are,' corrected Miss Menzies. 'What they are made of . . . surely not flesh and blood?'

'Surely not,' agreed Mr Pott. Then suddenly looked startled—a strange word echoed in his mind: had she said 'blood'? He laid down the inn-sign and turned to look at her. '*What* was you saying?' he asked.

Miss Menzies was away again. 'I was saying this lot couldn't be fairies—not on second thoughts and sober reflection. Why, this little fellow had a tear in his trousers and there he was—panting and puffing and toiling up the hill. There's another one in skirts—or maybe two in skirts. I can't make out how many there are; whether it's just one that keeps changing, or what it is. There was a little hand cleaning a window—rubbing and rubbing from the inside. But you couldn't see what it belonged to. White as a bluebell stalk, it looked, when you pull it out of the earth. And about that thickness—waving and swaying. And then I found my glasses and I saw it had an elbow. I could hardly believe my eyes. There it was, a cloth in its hand and going into the corners. And yet, in a way, it seemed natural.'

'In a way,' agreed Mr Pott. But he was looking rather lost.

CHAPTER FIVE

THEN BEGAN for Miss Menzies what afterwards seemed almost the happiest time of her life. She had always been a great watcher: she would watch ants in the grass, mice in the corn, spinnings of webs and buildings of nests. And she could keep very quiet, because, watching a spider plummet from a leaf, she would almost become a spider herself, and having studied the making of web after web she could have spun one herself to almost any shape, however awkward. Miss Menzies, in fact, had become quite critical of web-making.

'Oh, you silly thing . . .' she would breathe to the spider as it swayed in the air, '. . . not that leaf—it's going to fall. Try the thorn. . . .'

Now, sitting on the slope, her hands about her knees, she would watch the little people, screened—as she thought— by a tall clump of thistle. And everything she saw she described to Mr Pott.

'There are three of them,' she told him some days later, 'A mother, a father and a thin little girl. Difficult to tell their ages. Sometimes I think there's a fourth . . . something or someone who comes and goes. A shadowy sort of creature. But that, of course'—she sighed happily—'might just be my . . .'

'. . . fancy,' said Mr Pott.

'. . . imagination,' corrected Miss Menzies. 'It's strange, you know, that *you* haven't seen them!'

Mr Pott, busy brick-building, did not answer. He had decided the subject was human; village gossip of some kind, referring not to his Vine Cottage, but to the original one in Fordham.

'They've done wonders to the house,' Miss Menzies went on. 'The front door was stuck, you know. Warped, I suppose, with the rain. But he was working on it yesterday with a thing like a razor-blade. And there's another thing they've done. They've taken those curtains I made for your Crown and Anchor and put them up in Vine Cottage, so now you can't see inside. Not that I'd dare to look—you couldn't go that close, you see. And the High Street's so narrow. But isn't it exciting?'

Mr Pott grunted. Stirring his brick-dust and size, he frowned to himself and breathed rather heavily. Gossip about neighbours—he had never held with it. Nor, until now, had Miss Menzies. A talker, yes, but a lady born and bred. This wasn't like her, he thought unhappily . . . peeping in windows . . . no, it wasn't like her at all. She was on now about the station-master's coat.

'. . . she took it, you see. That's where it went. She took it for *him*, gold buttons and all, and he wears it in the evening, after sundown when the air gets chilly. I would not be at all surprised if, one day, she snapped up the vicar's cassock. It's so like a dress, you see, and would fit her perfectly. Except, of course, that might seem too obvious. They're very clever, you know. One would be bound to notice a vicar bereft of his cassock—there on the church steps for all to see. But to see the station-master you have to look right into the station. And you can't do that now; he could be without his coat for weeks and none of us any the wiser.'

Mr Pott stopped stirring to glare at Miss Menzies. She looked back in alarm at his round, angry eyes. 'But what is the matter?' she asked him uneasily, after a moment.

Mr Pott drew a deep breath. 'If you don't know,' he said, 'then I won't tell you!'

This did not seem very logical. Miss Menzies smiled forgivingly and laid a hand on his arm. 'But there's nothing to be frightened of,' she assured him; 'they're quite all right.'

He shook his arm free and went on stirring, breathing hard and clattering with his trowel. 'There's plenty to be frightened of,' he said sternly, 'when there's gossip on the tongue. Homes ruined, I've seen, and hearts broken.'

Miss Menzies was silent a moment. 'I didn't grudge her the coat,' she said at last. Mr Pott snorted and Miss Menzies went on: 'In fact, I intend to make them some clothes myself. I thought I'd just leave the clothes about for them to find, so they'll never know where they came from. . . .'

'That's better,' said Mr Pott, scraping at a brick. There was a long pause—so strangely long that Mr Pott became aware of it. Had he been a little too sharp, he wondered, and glanced sideways at Miss Menzies. With clasped knees, she sat smiling into space.

'I love them, you see,' she said softly.

After this Mr Pott let her talk again: if her interest stemmed from affection, that was another matter. Day after day he nodded and smiled, as Miss Menzies unfolded her story. The words spilled over him, soothing and gay, and slid away into the sunlight; very few caught his attention. Even on that momentous afternoon—one day in June— when, bursting with fresh news, she flung herself breathlessly beside him.

He was re-tarring a line of sleepers and, pot in one hand, brush in the other, he edged himself along the ground, his wooden leg stretched out before him. Miss Menzies, talking away, edged along to keep up with him.

'. . . and when she spoke to me,' gasped Miss Menzies, 'I was amazed, astounded! Wouldn't you have been?'

'Maybe,' said Mr Pott.

'This tiny creature—quite unafraid. Said she'd been watching me for weeks.'

'Get away,' said Mr Pott amiably. And he wiped a drop of tar off the rail. 'That's better,' he said, admiring the steely gleam. . . . 'Not a trace of rust anywhere,' he thought happily.

'And now I know what they're called and everything. They're called Borrowers . . .'

'Burroughs?' said Mr Pott.

'No, Borrowers.'

'Ah, Burroughs,' said Mr Pott, stirring the tar, which stood in a can of hot water. 'Getting a bit thick,' he thought, as he raised the stick and critically watched the trickle.

'It's not their family name,' Miss Menzies went on; 'their family name is Clock. It's their racial name—the kind of creatures they are. They live like mice . . . or birds . . . on what they can find, poor things. They're an offshoot of humans, I think, and live from human left-overs. They don't own anything at all. And of course they haven't any money. . . . Oh, it's perfectly all right,' said Miss Menzies, as in absent-minded sympathy Mr Pott clicked his tongue and gently shook his head. 'They wouldn't care about money. They wouldn't know what to do with it. But they have to live . . .'

'. . . and let live,' said Mr Pott brightly. He felt mildly pleased with this phrase and hoped it would fit in somewhere.

'But they *do* let live,' said Miss Menzies. 'They never take anything that matters. Except of course . . . well, I'm not sure about the station-master's overcoat. But when you come to think of it, the station-master didn't need it for warmth, did he? Being made as he is of barbola? And it wasn't his, either—I made it; come to that, I made *him*, too. So it really belongs to me. And I don't need it for warmth.'

'Not warmth,' agreed Mr Pott absently.

'These Borrowers do need warmth. They need fuel and shelter and water and they terribly need human beings. Not that they trust them. They're right, I suppose: one has only to read the papers. But it's sad, isn't it? That they can't trust us, I mean. What could be more charming for someone—like me, say—to share one's home with these little creatures? Not that I'm lonely, of course. My days'—Miss Menzies's eyes became over-bright suddenly and the gay voice hurried a little—'are *far* too full ever to be lonely. I've so many interests, you see. I keep up with things. And I have my old dog and the two little birds. All the same, it would be nice. I know their names now—Pod, Homily and Little Arrietty. These creatures talk, you see. And just think I'd'—she laughed suddenly—'I'd be sewing for them from morning until night. I'd make them things. I'd buy them things. I'd—oh, but you understand. . . .'

'I understand,' said Mr Pott. 'I get you. . . .' But he didn't understand. In a vague sort of way he felt it rather rude of Miss Menzies to refer to her new-found family of friends as 'creatures'. Down on their luck, they might be, but all the same . . . But then, of course, she did use the strangest expressions.

'And I think that's why she spoke to me,' Miss Menzies went on; 'she must have felt safe, you see. They always . . .'

'. . . know,' put in Mr Pott obligingly.

'Yes. Like animals and children and birds and . . . fairies.'

'I wouldn't commit meself about fairies,' said Mr Pott. And, come to think of it, he would not commit himself about animals, either: he thought of the badger whose life he had rescued—if *it* had 'known' he would still have had his leg.

'They've had an awful time, poor things, really ghastly. . . .' Miss Menzies gazed down the slope at the peaceful scene, the groups of miniature cottages, the smoking chimneys, the Norman church, the forge, the gleaming railway lines. 'It was wonderful, she told me, when they found this village'.

Mr Pott grunted. He shifted himself along a couple of feet and drew the tar-pot after him. Miss Menzies, lost in her dreams, did not seem to notice. Knees clasped, eyes half closed, she went on as though reciting.

'It was moonlight, she told me, the night they arrived. You can imagine it, can't you? The sharp shadows. They had heaps to carry and had to push their way up through those rushy grasses down by the water's edge. Spiller—that was the untamed one—took Arrietty round the village. He took her right inside the station, and there were those figures I made—the woman with the basket, the old man and the little girl—in a row on the seat, so still, so still . . . and just beside them the soldier with his kit-bag. They were speckled by moonlight and the fretted shadow of the station roof. They looked very real, she said, but like people under a spell or listening to music which neither she nor Spiller could hear. Arrietty too stood silent—staring and wondering at the pale moonlit faces. Until suddenly there was a rustling sound and a great black beetle ran right over them and she saw they were not alive. She doesn't mind beetles

herself, she rather likes them, but this one made her scream. She said there were toadstools in the ticket office, and when they went out of the station, the field-mice were busy in the High Street, running in and out of the shadows. And there, on the steps of the church, stood the vicar in his cassock— so silent, so still. And moonlight everywhere. . . .'

'Homily, of course, fell in love with Vine Cottage. And you can't blame her—it is rather charming. But the door was stuck, warped, I suppose, by the rain, and when they opened the window it seemed to be full of something and it smelled very damp. Spiller put his hand in and—do you know?—it was filled with white grass stalks, right up to the roof. White as mushrooms, they were, through growing up in the dark. So that night they slept out of doors.

'Next day, though, she said, was lovely—bright sunshine, spring smells and the first bee. They can see things so closely, you see: every hair of the bee, the depth of the velvet, the veins on its wings and the colours vibrating. The men'—Miss Menzies laughed—'I mean, you must call them men—soon cleared the cottage of weeds, reaping them down with a sliver of razor-blade and a kind of half nail-scissor. Then they dug out the roofs. Spiller found a chrysalis, which he gave to Arrietty. She kept it until last week. It turned out to be a red admiral. She watched it being born. But when its wings appeared and they began to see the size of it, there was absolute panic. Just in the nick of time they got it out of the front door. Its wing span would almost have filled their parlour from wall to wall. Imagine your own parlour full of butterfly and no way to let it out! When you come to think of it, it's quite fantas . . .'

'. . . tick,' added Mr Pott.

'About a week later they found your sandpile; and when they had dug up the floor they sanded it over and trod it down. Dancing and stamping like maniacs. She said it was rather fun. This was all in the very early morning. And about three weeks ago they borrowed your size. It was already mixed—when you were making that last lot of bricks, remember? Anyway, now what with sizing it over and one thing and another, she tells me, their floor has quite a good surface. They sweep it with thistle-heads. But it's early for these, she said, the blooms are too tightly packed. The ones which come later are far more practical . . .'

But Mr Pott had heard at last. 'My sand pile . . .' he said slowly, turning to stare at her.

'Yes.' Miss Menzies laughed. 'And your size.'

'My size?' repeated Mr Pott. He was silent a moment, as though thinking this out.

'Yes,' laughed Miss Menzies, 'but so little of it—so very, very little.'

'My size . . .' repeated Mr Pott. His face grew stern, almost belligerent he seemed suddenly as he turned to Miss Menzies.

'Where are these people?' he asked.

'But I've told you!' Miss Menzies exclaimed, and as he still looked angry, she took his horny hand in both of hers as though to help him up. 'Come,' she whispered, but she was still smiling, 'come very quietly, and I'll show you!'

CHAPTER SIX

'STILLNESS . . . that's the thing,' Pod whispered to Arrietty, the first time he saw Miss Menzies crouching down behind her thistle. 'They don't expect to see you, and if you're still they somehow don't. And never look at 'em direct—always look at 'em sideways like. Understand?'

'Yes, of course I understand—you've told me often enough. Stillness, stillness, quiet, quiet, creep, creep, crawl, crawl. . . . What's the good of being alive?'

'Hush,' said Pod and laid a hand on her arm. Arrietty had not been herself lately. It was as though, thought Pod, she had something on her mind. But it wasn't often she was as rude as this. He decided to ignore it: getting to the awkward age—that's what it was, he wouldn't wonder.

They stood in a clump of coarse grass, shoulder high to them, with only their heads emerging. 'You see,' breathed Pod, speaking with still lips out of the corner of his mouth, 'some kind of plant or flowers, that's what we look like to her. Something in bud, maybe.'

'Supposing she decided to pick us,' suggested Arrietty irritably. Her ankles were aching and she longed to sit down; ten minutes had become quarter of an hour and still neither party had moved. An ant climbed up the grass stem beside her, waved its antennae in the air and swiftly climbed down again. A slug lay sleeping under the plantain leaf, every now and again there was a slight ripple where the frilled underside of its body appeared to caress the earth.

'It must be dreaming,' Arrietty decided, admiring the silver highlights in the lustrous gun-metal skin. 'If my father were less old-fashioned', she thought guiltily, 'I would tell him about Miss Menzies, and then we could walk away.' But

35

in his view and in that of her mother it was still a disgrace to be 'seen', not only a disgrace but almost a tragedy; to them it meant broken homes, wearisome treks across unexplored country and the labour of building anew. By her parents' code, to be known to exist at all put their whole way of life into jeopardy, and a borrower once 'seen' must immediately move away.

In spite of all this, in her short life of fifteen years, Arrietty herself had been 'seen' four times. What was this longing, she wondered, which drew her so strongly to human beings?

And on this—her fourth occasion of being 'seen'—actually to speak to Miss Menzies? It was reckless and stupid, no doubt, but also strangely thrilling to address and be answered by a creature of so vast a size, who yet could seem so gentle; to see the giant eyes light up and the great mouth softly smile. Once you had done it and no dreadful disaster had followed, you were tempted to try it again. Arrietty had even gone so far as to lay in wait for Miss Menzies. Perhaps because every incident she described seemed so to delight and amaze her and—when Spiller was not there— Arrietty was often lonely.

Those first few days had been such wonderful fun! Spiller taking her on the trains—nipping into some half-empty carriage and, when the train moved, sitting so stiff and so still—pretending they too, like the rest of the passengers, were made of barbola wax. Round and round they would go, passing Vine Cottage a dozen times, and back again over the bridge. Other faces besides Mr Pott's stared down at them, and by Mr Pott's backdoor they saw rows of boots and shoes, fat legs, thin legs, stockinged legs and bare legs. They heard human laughter and human squeals of delight. It was terrifying and wonderful, but somehow, with Spiller, she felt safe. A plume of smoke ran out behind them. The

same kind of smoke which was used for the cottage chimneys, parcel string soaked in nitrate and secured in a bundle
by a twist of invisible hairpin. ('Have you seen my invisible
hairpins?' Miss Menzies had one day asked Mr Pott—a
question which to the puzzled Mr Pott seemed an odd
contradiction in terms.) In Vine Cottage, however, Pod had
hooked down the smouldering bundle and had lit a real fire
instead, which Homily fed with candle-grease, coal-slack
and tarry lumps of cinder. On this she cooked their meals.

And it was Spiller, wild Spiller, who had helped Arrietty
to make her garden and to search for plants of scarlet
pimpernel, small blue-faced bird's-eyes, fern-like mosses
and tiny flowering sedum. With Spiller's help she had
gravelled the path and laid a lawn of moss.

Miss Menzies, behind her thistle clump, had watched this
work with delight. She saw Arrietty; but Spiller, that past
master of invisibility, she could never quite discern. Both
still and swift, with a wild creature's instinct for cover, he
could melt into any background, and disappear at will.

With Spiller too Arrietty had explored the other houses,
fished for minnows and bathed in the river, screened by the
towering rushes. 'Getting too tomboyish by half,' Homily
had grumbled. She was nervous of Spiller's influence. 'He's
not our kind really,' she would complain to Pod, in a sudden
burst of ingratitude, 'even if he did save our lives.'

Standing beside her father in the grass and thinking of
these things, Arrietty began to feel the burden of her secret.
Had her parents searched the world over, she realized
uneasily, they could not have found a more perfect place in
which to settle—a complete village tailored to their size
and, with so much left behind by the visitors, unusually rich
in borrowings. It had been a long time since she had heard

her mother sing as she sang now at her housework, or her father take up again his breathy, tuneless whistle as he pottered about the village.

There was plenty of 'cover' but they hardly needed it. There was little difference in size between themselves and the borrowers made of wax and except during visiting hours Pod could walk about the streets quite freely, providing he was ready to freeze. And there was no end to the borrowing of clothes. Homily had a hat again at last and would never leave the house without it. 'Wait', she would say, 'while I put on my hat,' and took a fussed kind of joy in pronouncing the magic word. No, they could not be moved out now: that would be too cruel. Pod had even put a lock on the front door, complete with key. It was the lock of a pocket jewel-case belonging to Miss Menzies. He little knew to whom he owed this find—that she had dropped the case on purpose beside the clump of thistle to make the borrowing easy. And Arrietty could not tell him. Once he knew the truth (she had been through it all before), there would be worry, despair, recriminations and a pulling up of stakes.

'Oh dear, oh dear,' she breathed aloud unhappily, 'whatever should I do . . . ?'

Pod glanced at her sideways. 'Sink down,' he whispered, nudging her arm. 'She's turned her head away. Sink slowly into the grasses. . . .'

Arrietty was only too grateful to obey. Slowly their heads and shoulders lowered out of sight and after a moment's pause to wait and listen they crawled away among the grass stems, and taking swift cover by the churchyard wall they slid to safety through their own backdoor.

CHAPTER SEVEN

ONE DAY Miss Menzies began to talk back to Arrietty. At first her amazement had kept her silent, and confined her share of their conversations to the few leading questions which might draw Arrietty out. This for Miss Menzies was a most unusual state of affairs and could not last for long. As the summer wore on, she had garnered every detail of Arrietty's short life and a good deal of data besides. She had heard about the borrowed library of Victorian miniature books, through which Arrietty had learned to read and to gain some knowledge of the world. Miss Menzies, in her hurried, laughing, breathless way, helped to add to this knowledge. She began to tell Arrietty about her own girl-hood, her parents and her family home, which she always described as 'dear Gadstone'. She spoke of London dances and of how she had hated them; of someone called 'Aubrey', her closest and dearest friend—'my cousin, you see. We were almost brought up together. He would come to dear Gadstone for his holidays.' He and Miss Menzies would ride and talk and read poetry together. Arrietty, listening and learning about horses, wondered if there was any kind of animal which she could learn to ride. You could tame a mouse (as her cousin Eggletina had done), but a mouse was too small and too 'scuttley': you couldn't go far on a mouse. A rat? Oh no, a rat was out of the question. She doubted even if Spiller would be brave enough to train a rat. Fight one, yes—armed with Pod's old climbing-pin—Spiller was capable of that but not, she thought, of breaking a rat into harness. But what fun it would have been to go

riding with Spiller, as Miss Menzies had gone riding with
Aubrey.

'He married a girl called Mary Chumley-Gore,' said Miss
Menzies. 'She had very thick ankles.'

'Oh . . . !' exclaimed Arrietty.

'Why do you say "Oh" in that voice?'

'I thought he might have married you!'

Miss Menzies smiled and looked down at her hands. 'So
did I,' she said quietly. She was silent a moment and then she
sighed. 'I suppose he knew me too well. I was almost like a
sister.' She was quiet again as though thinking this out, and
then she added more cheerfully: 'They were happy though,
I gather; they had five children and lived in a house outside
Bath.'

And Miss Menzies, even before Arrietty explained to her,
understood about being 'seen'. 'You need never worry
about your parents,' she assured Arrietty. 'I would never—
even if you had not spoken—have looked at them directly.
As far as we are concerned—and I can speak for Mr Pott—
they are safe here for the rest of their lives. I would never
even have looked at you directly, Arrietty, if you had not
crept up and spoken to me. But even before I saw any of you
I had begun to wonder—because, you see, Arrietty, your
chimney sometimes smoked at quite the wrong sort of
times; I only light the string for the visitors, you see, and it
very soon burns out.'

'And you would never pick us up, any of us? In your
hands, I mean?'

Miss Menzies gave an almost scornful laugh. 'As though
I would dream of such a thing!' She sounded rather hurt.

Miss Menzies also understood about Spiller: that when he

came for his brief visits, with his offerings of nuts, corn grains, hard-boiled sparrows' eggs and other delicacies, she would not see so much of Arrietty. But after Spiller had gone again, she liked to hear of their adventures.

All in all, it was a happy, glorious summer for everyone concerned.

There were scares of course. Such as the footsteps before

dawn, human footsteps, but not those of the one-legged Mr Pott, when something or someone had fumbled at their door. And the moonlight night when the fox came, stalking silently down their village street, casting his great shadow and leaving his scent behind. The owl in the oak-tree was of course a constant source of danger. But, like most owls, he did his hunting farther afield, and once the vast shape had wafted over the river and they had heard his call on the other side of the valley, it was safe to sally forth.

Much of the borrowing was done at night before the mice got at the scraps dropped by the visitors. Homily at first had sniffed fastidiously when presented with, say, the remains of a large ham sandwich. Pod had to persuade her to look at the thing more practically—fresh bread, pure farm butter and a clean paper bag; what had been good enough for human beings should be good enough for them. What was wrong, he asked her, with the last three grapes of a stripped bunch? You could wash them, couldn't you, in the stream? You could peel them? Or what was wrong with a caramel, wrapped up in transparent paper? Half-eaten bath-buns, he agreed, were a bit more difficult . . . but you could extract the currants, couldn't you, and collect and boil down those crusted globules of sugar?

Soon they had evolved a routine of collecting, sorting, cleaning and conserving. They used Miss Menzies's shop as a storehouse, with—unknown to Pod and Homily—her full co-operation. She had cheated a little on the furnishings, having (some years ago now) gone into the local town and bought a toy grocer's shop, complete with scales, bottles, cans, barrels and glass containers. With these, she had skil-fully furnished the counter and dressed up the windows. This little shop was a great attraction to visitors—it was a general shop and post office modelled on the one in the village—bow windows, thatched roof and all. A replica of old Mrs Purbody (slimmed down a little to flatter her) stood behind the counter inside. Miss Menzies had even repro-duced the red knitted shawl which Mrs Purbody wore on her shoulders, both in summer and winter, and the crisp white apron below. Homily would borrow this apron when she worked on her sortings in the back of the shop, but would put it back punctually in time for visitors. Sometimes she washed it out, and every morning—regular as clock-work—she would dust and sweep the shop.

made a good deal of noise. They very soon
...is, however, and learned, in fact, to welcome it.
...: trains began to clatter and the smoke unfurled
...cottage chimneys, it warned them of Visiting
Hours. ...omily had time to take off the apron, let herself out
of the shop and cross the road to her home, where she
engaged herself in pleasant homely tasks until the trains
stopped and all was quiet again and the garden lay dreaming
and silent in the peaceful evening light.

Mr Pott, by this time, would have gone inside to his tea.

CHAPTER EIGHT

'THERE MUST be something we can do,' said Mrs Platter despairingly for about the fifth time within an hour. 'Look at the money we've sunk.'

'Sunk is the right word,' said Mr Platter.

'And it isn't as though we haven't tried.'

'Oh, we've tried hard enough,' said Mr Platter. 'And what annoys me about this Abel Pott is that he does it all without seeming to try at all. He doesn't seem to mind if people come or not. MODEL VILLAGE WITH LIVE INHABITANTS—that's what he'll put on the notice—and then we'll be finished. Finished for good and all! Better pack it in now, that's what I say, and sell out as a going concern.'

'There must be something . . .' repeated Mrs Platter stubbornly.

They sat as before at a green table on their singularly tidy lawn. On this Sunday evening it was even more singularly tidy than usual. Only five people had come that afternoon for RIVERSIDE TEAS. There had been three quite disastrous week-ends: on two of them it had rained, and on this particular Sunday there had been what local people spoke of as 'the aeronaut'—a balloon ascent from the fairground, with tea in tents, ice-cream, candy-floss and roundabouts. On Saturday people drove out to see the balloon itself (at sixpence a time to pass the rope barriers) and today in their hundreds to see the balloon go up. It had been a sad sight indeed for Mr and Mrs Platter to watch the carriages and motors stream past Ballyhoggin with never a glance nor a thought for RIVERSIDE TEAS. It had not comforted them either, when at about three o'clock in the afternoon the balloon itself sailed silently over them, barely clearing the

45

ilex tree which grew beside the house. They could even see 'the aeronaut', who was looking down—mockingly, it seemed—straight into the glaring eyes of Mr Platter.

'No good saying "there must be something",' he told her irritably. 'Night and day I've thought and thought and you've thought too. What with this balloon mania and Abel Pott's latest, we can't compete. That's all: it's quite simple. There isn't anything—short of stealing them.'

'What about that?' said Mrs Platter.

'About what?'

'Stealing them,' said Mrs Platter.

Mr Platter stared back at her He opened his mouth and shut it again. 'Oh, we couldn't do that,' he managed to say at last.

'Why not?' said Mrs Platter. 'He hasn't shown them yet. Nobody knows they're there.'

'Why, it would be—I mean, it's a felony.'

'Never mind,' said Mrs Platter, 'let's commit one.'

'Oh, Mabel,' gasped Mr Platter, 'what things you do say!' But he looked slightly awestruck and admiring.

'Other people commit them,' said Mrs Platter firmly, basking in the glow of his sudden approbation. 'Why shouldn't we?'

'Yes, I see your argument,' said Mr Platter. He still looked rather dazed.

'There's got to be a first time for everything,' Mrs Platter pointed out.

'But'—he swallowed nervously—'you go to prison for a felony. I don't mind a few extra items on a bill, I'm game for that, dear. Always was, as you well know. But this—oh, Mabel, it takes *you* to think of a thing like this!'

'Well, I said there'd be something,' acknowledged Mrs

Platter modestly. 'But it's only common sense, dear. We can't afford not to.'

'You're right,' said Mr Platter; 'we're driven to it. Not a soul could blame us.'

'Not a living soul!' agreed Mrs Platter solemnly in a bravely fervent voice.

Mr Platter leaned across the table and patted her hand. 'I take my hat off to you, Mabel, for courage and initiative. You're a wonderful woman,' he said.

'Thank you, dear,' said Mrs Platter.

'And now for ways and means . . .' said Mr Platter in a suddenly business-like voice. He took off his rimless glasses and thoughtfully began polishing them. 'Tools, transport, times of day. . . .'

'It's simple,' said Mrs Platter. 'You take the boat.'

'I realize that,' said Mr Platter with a kind of aloof patience. He put his rimless glasses back on his nose, returned the handkerchief to his pocket, leaned back in his chair and with the fingers of his right hand drummed lightly on the table. 'Allow me to think a while. . . .'

'Of course, Sidney,' said Mrs Platter obediently, and folded her hands in her lap.

After a few moments he cleared his throat and looked across at her. 'You'll have to come with me, dear,' he said.

Mrs Platter, startled, lost all her composure. 'Oh, I couldn't do that, Sidney. You know what I'm like on the water. Couldn't you take one of the men?'

He shook his head. 'Impossible, they'd talk.'

'What about Agnes Mercy?'

'Couldn't trust her, either; it would be all over the county before the week was out. No dear, it's got to be you.'

'I *would* come with you, Sidney,' faltered Mrs Platter,

'say we went round by road. That boat's kind of small for me.'

'You can't get into his garden from the road, except by going through the house. There's a thick holly hedge on either side with no sort of gate or opening. No, dear, I've got it all worked out in my mind: the only approach is by water. Just before dawn, I'd say, when they're all asleep, and that would include Abel Pott. We shall need a good strong cardboard box, the shrimping-net and a lantern. Have we any new wicks?'

'Yes, plenty up in the attic.'

'That's where we'll have to keep them—these . . . er . . . well, whatever they are.'

'In the attic?'

'Yes, I've thought it all out, Mabel. It's the only room we always keep locked —because of the stores and that. We've got to keep them warm and dry through the winter while we get their house built. They *are* part of the stores in a manner of speaking. I'll put a couple of bolts on the door, as well as the lock, and a steel plate across the bottom. That should

settle 'em. I've got to have time, you see,' Mr Platter went on earnestly, 'to think out some kind of house for them. It's got to be more like a cage than a house and yet it's got to *look* like a house, if you see what I mean. You've got to be able to see them inside and yet make it so they can't get out. It's going to take a lot of working on, Mabel.'

'You'll manage, dear,' Mrs Platter encouraged him. 'But'—she thought a moment—'what if *he* comes here and recognizes them? Anybody can buy a ticket.'

'He wouldn't. He's so taken up with his own things that I doubt if he's ever heard of us or of Ballyhoggin or even Went-le-Craye. But say he did? What proof has he? He's been keeping them dark, hasn't he? Nobody's seen them— or the news would be all over the county. In the papers most likely. People would be going there in hundreds. No, dear, it would be his word against ours—that's all. But we've got to act quickly, Mabel, and you've got to help me. There are two weeks left to the end of the season; he may be keeping them to show next year. Or he may decide to show them at once—and then we'd be finished. You see what I mean? There's no knowing . . .'

'Yes. . . .' said Mrs Platter. 'Well, what do you want me to do?'

'It's easy: you've only got to keep your head. I take the cardboard box and the lantern and you carry the shrimping-net. You follow me ashore and you tread where I tread, which you'll see by the lantern. I'll show you their house, and all you've got to do is to cover the rear side with the shrimping-net, holding it close as you can against the wall and partly over the thatch. Then I make some sort of noise at the front—they keep the front door locked now, I've found out that much. As soon as they hear me at the front door—

you can mark my words—they'll go scampering, out of the back. Straight into the net. You see what I mean? Now you'll have to keep the net held tight up against the cottage wall. I'll have the cardboard box in one hand by then, and the lid in the other. When I give the word, you scoop the net up into the air, with them inside it, and tumble them into the box. I clap the lid on and that will be that.'

'Yes,' said Mrs Platter uncertainly. She thought a while and then she said: 'Do they bite?'

'I don't know that. Only seen them from a distance. But it wouldn't be much of a bite.'

'Supposing one fell out of the net or something?'

'Well, you must see they don't, Mabel, that's all. I mean, there are only three or four of 'em, all told. We can't afford any losses. . . .'

'Oh, Sidney, I wish you could take one of the men. I can't even row.'

'You don't have to row. I'll row. All you have to do, Mabel, is to carry the net and follow me ashore. I'll point out their cottage and it'll be over in a minute. Before you can say Jack Robinson, we'll be back in the boat and safely home.'

'Does he keep a dog?'

'Abel Pott? No, dear, he doesn't keep a dog. It will be quite all right. Just trust me and do what I say. Like to come across to the island now and have a bit of practice on one of our own houses? You run up to the attic now and get the net and I'll get the oars and the boat-hook. Now, you've got to face up to it, Mabel,' added Mr Platter irritably, as Mrs Platter still seemed to hesitate; 'we must each do our part. Fair's fair, you know.'

CHAPTER NINE

THE NEXT day it began to rain and it rained on and off for ten days. Even Mr Pott had a falling-off of visitors. Not that he minded particularly; he and Miss Menzies employed themselves indoors at Mr Pott's long kitchen table—repairing, remodelling, repainting, restitching and oiling. . . . The lamplight shed its gentle glow around them. While the rain poured down outside, the glue-pot bubbled on the stove and the kettle sang beside it. At last came October the first, the day when the season ended.

'Mr Pott,' said Miss Menzies, after a short but breathy silence (she was quilting an eiderdown for Homily's double bed and found the work exacting), 'I am rather worried.'

'Oh,' said Mr Pott. He was making a fence of matchsticks, glueing them delicately with the aid of pincers and a fine sable brush. 'In fact', Miss Menzies went on, 'I'm very worried indeed. Could you listen a moment?'

This direct assault took Mr Pott by surprise. 'Something wrong?' he asked.

'Yes, I think something is wrong. I haven't seen Arrietty for three days. Have you?'

'Come to think of it, no,' said Mr Pott.

'Or any of them?'

Mr Pott was silent a moment, thinking back. 'Not now you mention it—no,' he said.

'I had an appointment with her on Monday, down by the stream, but she didn't turn up. But I wasn't worried, it was raining anyway and I thought perhaps Spiller had arrived. But he hadn't, you know. I know now where he keeps his

boat and it wasn't there. And then, when I passed their
cottage, I saw the backdoor was open. This isn't like them,
but it reassured me as I assumed they wouldn't be so care-
less unless they were all inside. When I passed again on my
way home for tea, the door was still open. All yesterday it
was open, and it was open again this morning. It's a bit . . .'

'. . . rum,' agreed Mr Pott.
'. . . odd,' said Miss Menzies—they spoke on the same
instant.
'Mr Pott, dear,' went on Miss Menzies, 'after I showed
them to you, so very carefully, you remember—you didn't
go and stare at them or anything? You didn't frighten
them?'
'No,' said Mr Pott, 'I been too busy closing up for
winter. I like to see 'em, mind, but I haven't had the time.'
'And their chimney isn't smoking,' Miss Menzies went

on. 'It hasn't been smoking for three days. I mean, one can't help being . . .'

'. . . worried,' said Mr Pott.

'. . . uneasy,' said Miss Menzies. She laid down her work. 'Are you still listening?' she asked.

Mr Pott tipped a matchstick with glue, breathing heavily. 'Yes, I'm thinking . . .' he said.

'I don't like to look right inside,' Miss Menzies explained. 'For one thing, you can't look in from the front because there's not room to kneel in the High Street, and you can't kneel down at the back without spoiling their garden, and the other thing is that, say they *are* inside—Pod and Homily, I mean—I'd be giving the whole game away. I've explained to you what they're like about being "seen"? If they hadn't gone already, they'd go then because I'd "seen" them. And we would be out of the frying-pan into the fire. . . .'

Mr Pott nodded; he was rather new to borrowers and depended on Miss Menzies for his data—she had, he felt—through months of study, somehow got the whole thing taped. 'Have you counted the people?' he suggested at last.

'Our people? Yes, I thought of that—and I've been through every one twice. A hundred and seven, and those two being mended. That's right, isn't it? And I've examined them all very carefully one by one and been through every railway carriage and everything. No, they're either in their house or they've gone right away. You're sure you didn't frighten them? Even by accident?'

'I've told you,' said Mr Pott. Very deliberately, he gave her a look, laid down his tools and went to the drawer in the table.

'What are you going to do?' asked Miss Menzies, aware that he had a plan.

'Find my screwdriver,' said Mr Pott. 'The roof of Vine Cottage comes off in a piece. It was so we could make the two floors—remember?'

'But you can't do that—supposing they *are* inside. It would be fatal!'

'We've got to take the risk,' said Mr Pott. 'Just get your coat on now and find the umbrella.'

Miss Menzies did as she was told; relieved, she felt suddenly, to surrender the leadership. Her father, she thought, would have acted just like this. And so, of course, would have Aubrey.

Obediently she followed him into the rain and held the umbrella while he went to work. Mr Pott took up a careful position within the High Street and Miss Menzies (feet awkwardly placed to avoid damage) teetered slightly above Church Lane and the back garden. Stooping anxiously they towered above the house.

Several deft turns of the screwdriver and a good deal of grunting soon loosened the soaking thatch. Lid-like, it came off in a piece. 'Bone dry inside,' remarked Mr Pott as he laid it aside.

They saw Pod and Homily's bedroom—a little bare it looked, in spite of the three pieces of doll's-house furniture which once Miss Menzies had bought and left about to be borrowed. The bed, with its handkerchief sheets, looked tousled as though they had left it hurriedly. Pod's working-coat, carefully folded, lay on a chair and his best suit hung on a safety-pin coat-hanger suspended against the wall; while Homily's day clothes were neatly ranged on two rails at the foot of the bed.

There was a feeling of deadness and desertion—no sound but the thrum of the rain as it pattered on the soaked umbrella.

Miss Menzies looked aghast. 'But this is dreadful—they've gone in their night clothes! What could have happened? It's like the *Marie Celeste*——'

'Nothing's been inside,' said Mr Pott, staring down, screwdriver in hand, 'no animal marks, no signs of what you'd call a scuffle. . . . Well, we better see what's below.

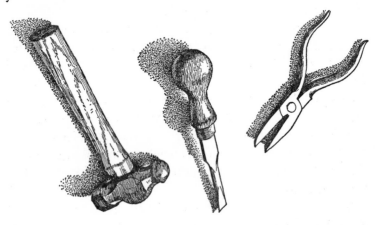

As far as I remember this floor comes out all in a piece with the stairs. Better get a box for the furniture.'

'The furniture!' thought Miss Menzies as she squelched back to the house, picking her way with great Gulliver-like strides over walls and railway lines, streets and alleyways. Just beside the churchyard her foot slipped on the mud, and to save herself she caught hold of the steeple; beautifully built, it held firm, but a bell rang faintly inside: a small, sad, ghostly protest. No; 'the furniture', she realized, was too grand an expression for the contents of that little room. If she had known she would have bought them more things, of left more about for them to borrow. She knew how clever they were at contriving but it takes time, she realized, to furnish a whole house from left-overs. She found a box at last and picked her way back to Mr Pott.

He had lifted out the bedroom floor with the ladder stairway attached and was gazing into the parlour. Neat but bare, Miss Menzies saw again: the usual match-box chest of drawers, a wood-block for a table, bottle-lid cooking-pots beside the hearth and Arrietty's truckle-bed pushed away in a corner; it was the deeper half of a velvet-lined case which must once have contained a large cigar-holder. She wondered where they had found it—perhaps Spiller had brought it to them? Here too the bedclothes had been thrown back hurriedly and Arrietty's day clothes lay neatly folded on a pill-box at the foot.

'I can't bear it,' said Miss Menzies in a stifled voice, feeling for her handkerchief. 'It's all right,' she went on hurriedly, wiping her eyes, 'I'm not going to break down. But what can we do? It's no good going to the police—they would only laugh at us in a polite kind of way and secretly think we were crazy. I know because of what happened when I saw that fairy. People would be polite to one's face, but . . .'

'I wouldn't know about fairies,' said Mr Pott, staring disconsolately into the gutted house, 'but *these* I seen with my own two eyes.'

'I am so glad and thankful that you did see them!' exclaimed Miss Menzies warmly, 'or where should I be now?' For once, it was almost a conversation.

'Well, we'll pack up these things,' said Mr Pott, suiting the action to the word, 'and set the roof back. Got to keep the place dry.'

'Yes,' said Miss Menzies, 'at least we can do that. Just in case . . .' her voice faltered and her fingers trembled a little, as carefully she took up the wardrobe. It had no hooks inside, she noticed—toymakers never quite completed things—so she laid it flat and packed it like a box with the little piles of clothes. The cheap piece of looking-glass flashed suddenly in a watery beam of sunlight and she saw the rain had stopped.

'Are we doing right?' she asked suddenly. 'I mean, shouldn't we leave it all as we found it? Supposing quite unexpectedly they did come back?'

Mr Pott looked thoughtful. 'Well,' he said, 'seeing as we got the place all opened up like, I thought maybe I'd make a few alterations.'

Miss Menzies, struggling with the rusty catch of Mr Pott's umbrella, paused to stare at him. 'You mean—make the whole place more comfortable?'

'That's what I do mean,' said Mr Pott. 'Do the whole thing over like—give them a proper cooking-stove, running water and all.'

'Running water! Could you do that?'

'Easy,' said Mr Pott.

The umbrella shut with a snap, showering them with drops, but Miss Menzies seemed not to notice. 'And I could furnish it,' she exclaimed; 'carpets, beds, chairs, everything. . . .'

'You got to do something,' said Mr Pott, eyeing her tear-marked face, 'to keep your mind off.'

'Yes, yes, of course,' said Miss Menzies.

'But don't be too hopeful about their coming back, you got to keep ready to face the worst. Say they had a fright and ran off on their own accord: that's one thing. Like as not, once the fright's over, they'd come back. But, say, they were *took*. Well, that's another matter altogether—

whoever it was that took them, took them to *keep* them, see what I mean?'

'*Whoever?*' repeated Miss Menzies wonderingly.

'See this,' said Mr Pott, moving aside his wooden leg and pointing with his screwdriver to a soggy patch in the High Street. 'That's a human footprint—and it's neither mine nor yours; the pavement's broken all along and the bridge is cracked as though someone has stood on it. Neither you nor me would do that, now would we?'

'No,' said Miss Menzies faintly. 'But', she went on wonderingly, 'no one except you and I knew of their existence.'

'Or so we thought,' said Mr Pott.

'I see,' said Miss Menzies, and was silent a moment.

Then she said slowly: 'I am thinking now, whether they laugh at us or not, I must report this loss to the police. It would stake our claim. In case', she went on, 'they should turn up somewhere else.'

Mr Pott looked thoughtful. 'Might be wise,' he said.

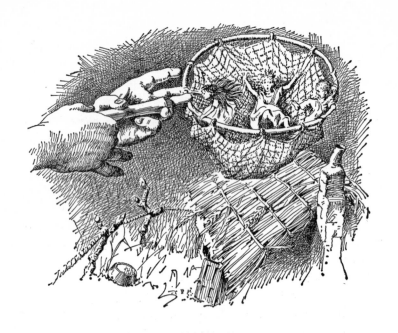

CHAPTER TEN

AT FIRST they lay very still in the corner of the cardboard box, recovering from the shock. Since the lid had been removed they were aware of vastness and of great, white, sloping ceilings. Two dormer windows, high in the tent-like walls, let in a coldish light. The edges of the box obscured the floor.

Arrietty felt very bruised and shaken: she glanced at her mother, who lay back limply, in her long white nightgown, her eyes still doggedly closed, and knew that, for the present, Homily had given up. She glanced at her father, who was leaning forward lost in thought, his hands limply on his knees, sat and noticed that he alone had managed to snatch up a garment—a patched pair of working trousers which he had pulled on over his nightshirt.

Shivering a little in her thin cambric nightgown, she crept towards him, and crouching beside him laid her cheek against his shoulder. He did not speak but his arm came loosely about her, and he patted her gently in an absent-minded way.

'Who are they?' she whispered huskily. 'What happened, Papa?'

'I don't rightly know,' he said.

'It was all so quick—like an earthquake. . . .'

'That's right,' he said.

'Mother won't speak,' whispered Arrietty.

'I don't blame her,' said Pod.

'But she's all right, I think,' Arrietty went on; 'it's just her nerves. . . .'

'We'd better take a look at her,' said Pod. They crawled towards her on their knees across the washed-out blanket with which the box was lined. For some reason—perhaps their old instinct for cover—neither as yet had dared stand upright.

'How are you feeling, Homily?' asked Pod.

'Just off dead,' she muttered faintly through barely moving lips. Dreadful she looked—lying so straight and so still.

'Anything broken?' asked Pod.

'Everything,' she moaned. But when anxiously he tried to feel the stick-like arms and fragile outstretched legs, she sat up suddenly and exclaimed crossly: 'Don't, Pod,' and began to pin up her hair. She then sank back again, and in a faint voice murmured: 'Where am I?' and with a loose, almost tragic gesture, flung the back of her hand on her brow.

'Well, we could all ask ourselves *that*,' said Pod. 'We're

in some kind of room in some kind of human house.' He glanced up at the distant windows. 'We're in an attic; that's where we are. Take a look . . .'

'I couldn't,' said Homily, and shivered.

'And we're alone,' said Pod.

'We won't be for long,' said Homily. 'I've got my "feeling", and I've got it pretty sharp.'

'She's right,' said Arrietty, and gripped her father's shoulder. 'Listen!'

With beating hearts and raised faces they crouched together tensely in the corner of the box—there were footsteps below them on the stairs.

Arrietty sprang up wildly but her father caught her by the arm. 'Steady, girl, what are you after?'

'Cover,' gasped Arrietty, as the footsteps became less muffled. 'There must be somewhere. . . . Come on, quick, let's hide!'

'No good,' said Pod; 'they know we're here. There'd only be searchings and pokings and sticks and pullings-out; your mother couldn't stand it. No, better we stay dead quiet.'

'But we don't know what they'll do to us,' Arrietty almost sobbed. 'We can't just be here and let them!'

Homily suddenly sat up and took Arrietty in her arms. 'Hush, girl, hush,' she whispered, strangely calm all at once. 'Your father's right. There's nothing we can do.'

The footsteps grew louder as though the stairs were now uncarpeted, and there was a creaking of wooden treads. The borrowers clung more tightly together. Pod, face raised, was listening intently.

'That's good,' he breathed in Arrietty's ear. 'I like to hear that—gives us plenty of warning—they can't burst in on us unexpected like.'

Arrietty, still sobbing below her breath, clung to her mother's waist—never had she been more terrified. 'Hush, girl, hush . . .' Homily kept saying.

The footsteps now had reached the landing. There was

heavy breathing outside the door, the clink of keys and the tinkle of china. There was the thud of a drawn bolt; and then another, and a key squeaked and turned in the lock.

'Careful,' said a voice; 'you're spilling it!'

Then the floorboards creaked and trembled as the two pairs of footsteps approached. A great plate loomed suddenly over them, and behind the plate, a face. Extraordinary it looked—pink and powdered, with piled-up golden hair, on each side of this face two jet earrings dangled towards them. Down it came, closer, closer—until they could see

each purple vein in the powdered bloom of the cheeks and
each pale eyelash of the staring light-blue eyes; and the
plate was set down on the floor.

Another face appeared hanging beside the first—tighter
and lighter, with rimless glasses, blank and pale with light.
A saucer swung sharply towards them and was set down
beside the plate.

The pinkish mouth of the first face opened suddenly and
some words came tumbling out. 'Think they're all right,
dear?' it said—on a warm gust of breath which ruffled
Homily's hair.

From the other face they saw the rimless glasses removed
suddenly, polished and put back again. Scared as he was,
Pod could not help thinking: 'I could use those for something, and that great silk handkerchief, too.' 'Bit out of
shape,' the thinner mouth replied; 'you bumped them a bit
in the box.'

'What about a drop of brandy in their milk, dear?'
the pink mouth suggested. 'Have you got your hip
flask?'

The rimless glasses receded, disappeared for a moment
and there was the clink of metal on china. Pod, in some
message to Homily, tightened his grip on her hand. Quite
strongly, she squeezed his back as the first voice said:
'That's enough, Sidney, you don't want to overdo it.'

Again the two faces loomed over them, staring,
staring. . . .

'Look at their little faces—hands, hair, feet and everything. What *are* they, do you think, Sidney?'

'They're a find, that's what they are! They're a gold-
mine! Come, dear, they won't eat while we're here.'

'Suppose I picked one up?'

'No, Mabel, they shouldn't be handled.' (Again Pod squeezed Homily's hand.)

'How do you know?'

'It stands to reason—we haven't got them here as pets. Leave them be now, Mabel—and let's see how they settle. We can come back a bit later on.'

CHAPTER ELEVEN

'MABEL AND SIDNEY,' said Arrietty, as the footsteps died away. She seemed quite calm suddenly.

'What do you mean?' asked Pod.

'Those are their names,' said Arrietty lightly. 'Didn't you listen when they were talking?'

'Yes, I heard them say that we mustn't be handled and they would put a drop of brandy in our milk . . .'

'As though we were cats or something!' muttered Homily.

But suddenly they all felt relieved; the moment of terror had passed—at least they had seen their captors.

'If you ask me,' said Pod, 'I'd say they were not too bright. Clever enough maybe, in their way—but not what you'd rightly call "bright".'

'Mabel and Sidney?' said Arrietty. She laughed suddenly and walked to the edge of the box.

Pod smiled at her tone. 'Yes, them,' he said.

'Food,' announced Arrietty, looking out over the box edge. 'I'm terribly hungry, aren't you?'

'I couldn't touch a thing!' said Homily. But after a moment she seemed to change her mind. 'What *is* there?' she asked faintly.

'I can't quite recognize it from here,' Arrietty told her, leaning over.

'Wait a moment,' said Pod, 'something's just come to me —something important, and it's come to me like a flash. Come back here, Arrietty, sit down beside your mother— the food won't run away.'

When both were seated, waiting expectantly, Pod

coughed to clear his throat. 'We don't want to underrate our position,' he began. 'I been thinking it over and I don't want to frighten you like—but our position is bad, it's very bad indeed.' He paused, and Homily took Arrietty's hand in both of hers and patted it reassuringly, but her eyes were on Pod's face. 'No borrower,' Pod went on, 'at least none that I've ever heard tell of—has lived in the absolute power of a set of human beings. The absolute power!' he repeated, gravely, looking from one scared face to the other. 'Borrowers have been "seen"—we've been "seen" ourselves—borrowers have been starved out or chased away—but I never heard tell of this sort of caper—not ever in the whole of my life. Have you, Homily?'

Homily moistened her lips. 'No,' she whispered. Arrietty looked very grave.

'Well, unless we can hit on some sensible way of escape that's what's going to happen to us. We're going to live out our lives in the absolute power of a set of human beings. The absolute power. . . .' he repeated again slowly as though to brand the phrase on their minds. There was an awed silence, until Pod spoke again 'Now, who is the captain of our little ship?'

'You are, Pod,' said Homily huskily.

'Yes, I am. And I'm going to ask a lot of you both—and I'm going to make rules as we go—depending on what's needed. The first rule, of course, is obedience. . . .'

'That's right,' nodded Homily, squeezing Arrietty's hand.

'. . . And the second rule—this is the thing that came to me—is: we must none of us speak a word.'

'Now, Pod . . .' began Homily reasonably, aware of her own limitations.

Arrietty saw the point. 'He means to Mabel and Sidney.'

Pod smiled again at her tone, albeit rather wryly. 'Yes, them,' he said. 'Never let 'em know we can speak. Because' —he struck his left palm with two fingers of his right to emphasize his meaning—'if they don't think we can speak, they'll think we don't understand. Just as they are with animals. And if they think we don't understand, they'll talk before us. *Now* do you get my meaning?'

Homily nodded several times in quick succession: she felt very proud of Pod.

'Well,' he went on in a more relaxed tone, 'let's take a look at this food, and after we've eaten we're going to begin a tour of this room—explore every crack and cranny of it from floor to ceiling. May take us several days. . . .'

Arrietty helped her mother to her feet. Pod, at the box edge, swung a leg and lightly dropped to the floor. Then he turned to help Homily. Arrietty followed and made at once for the plate.

'Cold rice pudding,' she said, walking round it, 'a bit of mince, cold cabbage, bread'—she put out a finger to touch something black, she sucked the finger—'and half a pickled walnut.'

'Careful, Arrietty,' warned Homily, 'it may be poisoned.'

'I wouldn't reckon so,' said Pod. 'Seems like they want us alive. Wish I knew for why.'

'But how are we supposed to drink this milk?' complained Homily.

'Well, take it up in your hands, like.'

Homily knelt down and cupped her hands. Her face became very milky but as she drank a reviving warmth seemed to flow through her veins, and her spirits lifted.

'Brandy,' she said. 'Back home at Firbank they kept it in the morning room and those Overmantels used to——'

'Now, Homily,' said Pod, 'this is no time for gossip. And that was whisky.'

'Something anyway, and dead drunk they used to be— or so they say—every time the bailiff came in to do the accounts. What's the mince like, Arrietty?'

'It's good,' she replied, licking her fingers.

CHAPTER TWELVE

'Now', said Pod some time later when they had finished eating, 'we better start on the room.'

He looked upwards. In each sharply sloping wall was set a dormer window, at what seemed a dizzy height; the windows were casement-latched and each had a vertical bolt. Above each was a naked curtain rail, hung with rusted rings. Through one window Pod could see the bough of an ilex-tree tossing in the wind.

'It's odd', Arrietty remarked, 'how from starting under the floor we seem to get higher and higher. . . .'

'And it isn't natural', put in Homily quickly, 'for borrowers to get high. Never leads to no good. Look at those Overmantels, for instance, back in the morning room at Firbank. Stuck up they were, through living high. Never so much as give you good day, say you were on the floor. It was as though they couldn't see you. Those windows are no good,' she remarked, 'doubt if even a human being could reach up there. Wonder how they clean them?'

'They'd stand on a chair,' said Pod.

'What about the gas-fire?' Homily suggested.

'No hope there,' said Pod, 'it's soldered into the chimney surround.'

It was a small iron gas-fire, with a separate ring— on which, in a pan, stood a battered glue-pot.

'What about the door?' said Arrietty. 'Suppose we cut a piece out of the bottom?'

'What with?' asked Pod, who was still examining the fireplace.

'We might find something,' said Arrietty, looking about her.

There were plenty of objects in the room. Beside the fireplace stood a dressmaker's dummy, upholstered in a dark green rep: it was shaped like an hourglass, had a knob

for a head and below the swelling hips a kind of wire-frame
petticoat—a support for the fitting of skirts. It stood on
three curved legs with swivel wheels. Its dark green bosom
was stuck with pins and on one shoulder, in a row, three
threaded needles. Arrietty had a strange thought: did
human beings look like this, she wondered, without their
clothes? Were they, unlike the borrowers, perhaps not made
of flesh and blood at all? Come to think of it, as 'Mabel' had
put down the plate, there had been a kind of creaking; and it
stood to reason that, to keep such bulk erect, there must
surely be some hidden form of scaffolding.

Above the mantel-shelf, on either side, were swivel gas-
brackets of tarnished brass. From one hung a length of
measuring tape, marked in inches. On the shelf itself she
saw the edge of a chipped saucer, the blades of what must
be a pair of cutting-out scissors, and a large iron horseshoe
propped upside down.

At right angles to the fireplace, pulled out from the
sloping wall, she saw a treadle sewing-machine; it was like
one she remembered at Firbank. Above the sewing-machine,
hanging on a nail, were the inner tube of a bicycle tyre and
a bunch of raffia. There were two trunks, several piles of
magazines and some broken slatted chairs. Between the
trunks, leaning at an angle, was the shrimping-net which had
achieved their capture. Homily glanced at the bamboo
handle and, shuddering, averted her eyes.

On the other side of the room, a fair-sized kitchen table
was pushed against the wall, and beside it a ladder-back
chair. The table was piled with various neat stacks of plates
and saucers, and other things which from floor level were
difficult to recognize.

On the floor, beyond the chair and immediately below the

window, stood a solid box of walnut veneer, inlaid with tarnished brass. The veneer was cracked and peeling. 'It's a dressing-case,' said Pod, who had seen something like it at Firbank, 'or one of those folding writing-desks. No, it isn't though,' he went on as he walked round to the far side, 'it's got a handle. . . .'

'It's a musical-box,' said Arrietty.

After a moment of seeming stuck, the handle wound quite easily. They could turn it as one turned an old-fashioned mangle, though the upward swing at its highest limit was difficult to control. Homily could manage, though, with her long wrists and arms; she was a little taller than Pod. There was a grinding sound from within the box and suddenly the tune tinkled out. It was fairylike and charming, but somehow a little sad. It ended very abruptly.

'Oh, play it again!' cried Arrietty.

'No, that's enough,' said Pod, 'we've got to get on.' He was staring towards the table.

'Just once,' pleaded Arrietty.

'All right,' he said, 'but hurry up. We haven't got all day. . . .'

And while they played their encore he stood in the middle of the room, gazing thoughtfully at the table top.

When at last they came beside him, he said: 'It's worth while getting up there!'

'Don't see quite how you could,' said Homily.

'Quiet,' said Pod, 'I'm getting it. . . .'

Obediently they stood silent, watching the direction of his eyes as he gauged the height of the ladder-back chair, and then, turning his back on it, glanced up at the raffia on the opposite wall, took in the position of the pins in the bosom of the dressmaker's dummy, and turned back again to the table. Homily and Arrietty held their breaths, aware some great issue was at stake.

'Easy,' said Pod at last, 'child's play,' and, smiling, he rubbed his hands: it always cheered him to solve a professional problem. 'Some good stuff up there, I shouldn't wonder.'

'But what good can it do us?' asked Homily, 'seeing there's no way out?'

'Well, you never know,' said Pod. 'Anyway,' he went on briskly, 'keeps your hand in and your mind off.'

CHAPTER THIRTEEN

THE NEXT two or three days established their daily routine. At about nine o'clock each morning Mr or Mrs Platter—or both—would arrive with their food. They would air the attic, clear away the dirty plates and generally set the borrowers up for the day. Mrs Platter—to Homily's fury, persisted with the cat treatment: a saucer of milk, a bowl of water and a baking tin of ashes, set out daily beside their food on a clean sheet of newspaper.

Towards evening, at between six and seven o'clock, the process was repeated and was called 'putting them to bed'. It was dark by then and sometimes they would have dozed off—to be woken suddenly by the scrape of a match and the flare of a roaring gas-jet. It was one of Pod's rules that, however active they might be between whiles, the Platters' arrival should always find them once again in their box. The footsteps on the stairs gave them plenty of warning. 'And never let them know we can climb.'

The morning food seemed to consist of the remains of the Platters' breakfast; the evening food, the remains of the Platters' midday meal, was slightly more interesting. Anything they left on the plate was never served up again. 'After all,' they had heard Mr Platter say, 'there are no books about them, no way to find out what they live on except by trial and error. We must try them out with a bit of this and that, and we'll soon see what agrees.'

Except on the rare occasions when Mr or Mrs Platter decided to do a repairing job in the attic or to stagger upstairs with trays of china or cutlery to be put away for the winter, the hours between meals were their own.

They were very active hours. On that first afternoon Pod, with the aid of a bent pin and a knotted strand of raffia, achieved the ascent of the table, and once safely ensconced, showed Arrietty how to follow. Later, he said, they would make a raffia ladder.

Gradually they worked their way through various cardboard boxes; some contained teaspoons and cutlery; some contained paper windmills, others toy balloons. There were boxes of nails and assorted screws and there was a small square biscuit-tin without a lid, filled with a jumble of keys. There was a tottering pile of pink-stained strawberry baskets and there were sets of neatly packed ice-cream cones, hermetically sealed in transparent grease-proof paper.

There were two drawers in the table, one of which was not quite closed. They squeezed through the crack, and in the half light saw it was full of tools. Pod's leg went down between a spanner and a screwdriver, in extricating which he rolled the screwdriver over and struck Arrietty on the ankle. Although neither injury was serious, they decided the drawer was a dangerous place and put it out of bounds.

By the fourth day the operation was complete: they had learned the position and possible use of every object in the room. They had even succeeded in opening the lid of the musical-box, in a vain hope of changing the tune. It slid up quite easily on a brass arm which, clinking into a locked position, held the lid in place. It closed, rather faster but almost as easily, by pressure on a knob. They could not change the tune, however; the brass cylinders, spiked with an odd pattern of steel prickles, were too heavy for them to lift, and they could only look longingly at the five unknown tunes on the equally heavy cylinders ranged at the back of the box. But with each new discovery—such as the steel

backing of the lower part of the door and the dizzy height of
the dormer windows from which the
sloping walls slid steeply away—their
hopes grew fainter: there still seemed
no way of escape.

Pod spent more and more of his time
just sitting and thinking. Arrietty, tired
of the musical-box, had discovered on
the magazine pile several tattered copies
of the *Illustrated London News*. She
would drag them one at a time under
the table, and turning over the vast sail-
like pages would walk about on them
listlessly, looking at the pictures and
sometimes reading aloud.

'You see nobody knows where we
are,' Pod would exclaim, breaking a
dreary silence, 'not even Spiller.'

'And not even Miss Menzies . . .'
Arrietty would think to herself, staring
unhappily at a half-page diagram of a
dam to be built on the lower reaches of
the Nile.

As the mornings became chillier
Homily tore some strips off the worn
blanket and she and Arrietty fashioned
themselves   sarong-like
skirts and pointed shawls to
draw round their shoulders.

Seeing this, the Platters
decided to light the gas-fire
and would leave it burning

low. The borrowers were glad, because, although sometimes the air grew dry and stuffy, they were able to toast
up scraps of the duller foods and make their meals more
appetizing.

One day Mrs Platter bustled in and, looking very purpose-
ful, went to the closed drawer of the table. Watching her
from their box in the corner as she pulled out some of the
contents they saw it contained rags and rolls of old stuff,
neatly tied round with tape. She unrolled a piece of yellowed
flannel and, taking up the cutting-out scissors, came and
stared down on them with narrowed, thoughtful eyes.

They stared back nervously at the waving scissor blades.
Was she going to snip and snap and tailor them to size?
But no—with a little creaking and much heavy breathing,
she kneeled down on the floor and, spreading the stuff
doubled before her, cut out three combination garments,
each one all of a piece, with magyar sleeves and legs. These
she seamed up on the sewing-machine, 'tutting' to herself
under her breath when the wheel stuck or the thread parted.
When her thimble rolled away under the treadle of the
sewing-machine they noted its position: a drinking-cup
at last!

Breathing hard, and with the aid of a bone crochet-hook,
Mrs Platter turned the garments inside out. 'There you
are,' she said, and threw them into the box. They lay there
stiffly like little headless effigies. None of the borrowers
moved.

'You can put them on yourselves, can't you?' said Mrs
Platter at last. The borrowers stared back at her, with wide,
unblinking eyes, until, after waiting a moment, she turned
and went away.

They were terrible garments, stiff and shapeless, fitting

nowhere at all. But at least they were warm; and Homily could now rinse out their own clothes in the bowl of drinking water and hang them before the gas-fire to dry. 'Thank heavens, I can't see myself,' she remarked grimly, as she gazed incredulously at Pod.

'Thank goodness you can't,' he replied, smiling, and he turned rather quickly away.

CHAPTER FOURTEEN

As THE weeks went by they learned gradually of the reason for their capture and the use to which they would be put. As well as the construction of the cage-like house on the island, Mr and Mrs Platter—assured of vast takings at last—were installing a turnstile in place of the gate to the drive.

One side of their cage-house, they learned, was to be made of thick plate-glass, exposing their home life to view. 'Good and heavy' the glass would have to be—Mr Platter had insisted, describing the 'layout' to Mrs Platter—nothing the borrowers could break; and fixed in a slot so the Platters could raise it for cleaning. The furniture was to be fixed to the floor and set in such a way that there should be nothing behind which they might hide.

'You know those cages at the Zoo with sleeping-quarters at the back, where you wait and wait, and the animal never comes out? Well, we don't want anything like that. Can't have people asking for their money back. . . .'

Mrs Platter had agreed. She saw the whole project in her mind's eye and thought Mr Platter very far-seeing and wonderful. 'And you've got to set the cage,' he went on earnestly, 'or house, or whatever we decide to call it, in a bed of cement. You can't have them burrowing.'

No, that wouldn't do, Mrs Platter had agreed again. And as Mr Platter went ahead with the construction of the house, Mrs Platter, they learned, had arranged with a seamstress to make them an entirely new wardrobe. She had taken away their own clothes to serve as patterns for size. Homily was

very intrigued by Mrs Platter's description to Mr Platter of
a green dress 'with a hint of a bustle—like my purple plaid,
you remember?' 'Wish I could *see* her purple plaid,' Homily
kept worrying, 'just so as to get the idea. . . .'

But Pod's thoughts were set on graver matters. Every
conversation overheard brought day by day an increasing
awareness of their fate: to live out the rest of their lives

under a barrage of human eyes—a constant, unremitting
state of being 'seen'. Flesh and blood could not stand it, he
thought; they would shrivel up under these stares—that's
what would happen—they would waste away and die. And
people would watch them even on their deathbeds—they
would watch, with necks craned and shoulders jostling—
while Pod stroked the dying Homily's brow or Homily
stroked the dying Pod's. No, he decided grimly, from now
on there could be but one thought governing their lives—
a burning resolve to escape: to escape while they were still
in the attic; to escape before spring. Cost what it might, he

realized, they must never be taken alive to that house with a wall of glass!

For these reasons, as the winter wore on, he became irritated by Homily's fussings over details such as the ash-pan and Arrietty's unheeding preoccupation with the *Illustrated London News*.

CHAPTER FIFTEEN

DURING THIS period (mid November to December) several projects were planned and attempted. Pod had succeeded in drawing out four nails which secured a patch of mended floorboard below the kitchen table. 'They don't walk here, you see,' he explained to his wife and child, 'and it's in shadow like.' These four stout nails he replaced with slimmer ones from the tin box on the table. The finer nails could be lifted out with ease and the three of them together could move the boards aside. Below they found the familiar joists and crossbeams, with a film of dust which lay—ankle-deep to them—on the ceiling plaster of the room below. ('Reminds me of the time when we first moved in under the floor at Firbank,' said Homily. 'I thought sometimes we would never get it straight, but we did.')

But Pod's project was nothing to do with home-making—he was seeking a way which might lead them to the lath and plaster walls of the room immediately below. If they could achieve this, he thought, there was nothing to stop them climbing down through the whole depth of the house, with the help of the laths within the walls: mice did it, rats did it; and as he pointed out, risky and toilsome as it was, they had done it several times themselves. ('We were younger then, Pod,' Homily reminded him nervously, but she seemed quite willing to try.)

It was no good, however; the attic was in the roof and the roof was set fairly and squarely on the brickwork of the main house, bedded and held in some mixture like cement. There was no way down to the laths.

Pod's next idea was one of breaking a small hole in the plaster of the ceiling below, and with the aid of the swinging ladder made of raffia, descend without cover into whatever room it might turn out to be.

'At least', he said, 'we'd be one floor down, the window will be lower and the door unlocked. . . .' First, though, he decided to borrow a packing-needle from the tool drawer and make a peephole. This, too, was hazardous: not only might the ceiling crack but there was bound to be some small fall of plaster on to the floor below. They decided to risk it, however; borrowers' eyes are particularly sharp: they could manage with a very small hole.

When at last they had made the hole and to their startled gaze the room below sprang to view, it turned out to be Mr and Mrs Platter's bedroom. There was a large brass bed, a very pink, shiny eiderdown, a Turkey carpet, a wash-hand-stand with two sets of flowered china, a dressing-table and a cat-basket. And what was still more alarming, Mrs Platter was having her afternoon's rest. It was an extraordinary sight to see her vast bulk from this angle, propped against the pillows. Very peaceful and unconcerned she looked, reading a home journal—leisurely turning the pages and eating butterscotch from a round tin. The cat lay on the eiderdown at her feet. A powdery film of ceiling plaster had settled in a ring on the pinkness of the eiderdown just beside the cat. This, Pod realized thankfully, would be swiftly shaken off when Mrs Platter arose.

Trembling and silent the borrowers backed away from their peephole, and noiselessly felt their way through the blanketing dust to the exit in the floorboards. Silently they lifted the small plank into place and gingerly dropped back the nails.

'Phew! . . .' said Pod, sinking back, as they reached their box in the corner. He wiped his brow on his sleeve, 'didn't expect to see that!' He looked very shaken.

'Nor did I,' said Homily. She thought a while. 'But it might be useful.'

'Might,' agreed Pod uncertainly.

The next attempt concerned the window—the one through which they could see the waving branch of the ilex. This branch was their only link with out of doors. 'Wind's in the east today,' Mrs Platter would sometimes say as she opened the casements to air the attic—this she achieved by standing on a chair—and the borrowers took note of what she said, and by the streaming of the leaves in one direction or another could roughly foretell the weather: 'wind in the east' meant snow.

When the flakes piled up on the outer sill they liked to watch them dance and scurry, but were thankful for the gas-fire. This was early January and not the most auspicious weather for Pod's study of the window, but they had no time to lose.

Homily, on occasion, was apt to discourage him. 'Say we did get it open, where would we be? On the roof! And you can see how steep it is by the slope of these ceilings. I mean, we're better in here than on the roof, Pod. I'm game in most things, but if you think I'm going to make a jump for that branch, you'll have to think again.'

'You couldn't make a jump for that branch, Homily,' Pod would tell her patiently, 'it's yards and yards away. And what's more, it's never still. No, it's not the branch I'm thinking of . . .'

'What are you thinking of, then?'

'Of where we are,' said Pod, 'that's what I want to find out. You might *see* something from the roof. You've heard them talk—about Little Fordham and that. And about the river. I'd like just to know where we *are*.'

'What good does that do us', retorted Homily, 'if we can't get out, anyway?'

Pod turned and looked at her. 'We've got to keep trying,' he explained.

'I know, Pod,' admitted Homily quickly. She glanced towards the table, under which, as usual, Arrietty was immersed in the *Illustrated London News*, 'and we both want to help you. I mean, we did make the raffia ladder. Just tell us what to do.'

'There isn't much you *can* do,' said Pod, 'at least not at the moment. What foxes me about this window is that, to free the latch you have to turn the handle of the catch upwards. See what I mean? The same with that vertical bolt—you've got to pull it out of its socket *upwards*. Now say to open the window you had to turn the handle of the catch downwards—that would be easy! We could fling a piece of twine or something over, swing our weight on the twine like and the catch would slide up free.'

'Yes,' said Homily thoughtfully, staring at the window. 'Yes, I see what you mean.' They were silent a moment— both thinking hard. 'What about that curtain rod?' asked Homily at last.

'The curtain rod? I don't quite get you. . . .'

'Is it fast in the wall?'

Pod screwed up his eyes. 'Pretty fast, I'd say, it's brass. And with those brackets . . .'

'Could you get a bit of twine over the curtain rod?'

'Over the curtain rod?'

'Yes, and use it like a pulley.'

A change came over Pod's face. 'Homily,' he said, 'that's it! Here am I—been weeks on the problem . . . and you hit on the answer first time. . . .'

'It's nothing,' said Homily, smiling.

Pod gave his orders; and swiftly they all went to work: the ball of twine and a small key to be carried to the table and up to the topmost box (this to bring Pod, sideways on, to within easier throwing distance of the curtain rod); the horseshoe to be knocked from the mantel-shelf to the floor, and to be dragged to a spot beside the musical-box, and immediately below the window; several patient swinging throws by Pod from the box pile on the table of the key attached to the twine, aimed at the wall above the curtain rod, which stood out slightly on its twin brass brackets (and suddenly there had been the welcome clatter of the key against the glass and the key falling swiftly as Arrietty paid out the twine—down past the window, past the sill, to Homily on the floor, beside the horseshoe); the removal of the key by Homily and the knotting of the raffia ladder to the twine to be wound back again by Arrietty, to bring the head of the ladder even with the window catch; the tying, by Homily, of the base of the swinging ladder to the horseshoe on the floor; the twine to be pulled taut and made fast by Arrietty to a table leg; the descent of Pod to the floor.

It was wonderful. The ladder rose tautly from the horseshoe, straight up the centre join of the casement windows to the catch, held firmly by the twine around the curtain rod.

Up the raffia ladder went Pod, watched by Arrietty and Homily from the floor. When on a level with the window catch, he hooked the first rung over the curtain rail, making —for a few essential moments—the ladder independent of the twine. Arrietty, beside the table leg, paying out several inches from the ball, enabling Pod to knot the twine about the iron handle of the catch. Pod then descending to the floor from the table leg and bringing the ball directly below the window.

'So far, so good,' he said. 'Now we've all got to pull on the twine. You behind Arrietty, Homily, and I'll bring up the rear.'

Obediently they did as he said. With a twist of twine tug-of-war-like around each tiny fist, they leaned backwards into the room, panting and straining and digging in their heels. Slowly, steadily the handle of the latch moved upward and the hammer-shaped head dipped down in a sliding half-circle, until at last it left one casement free.

'We've done it,' said Pod. 'You can let go now. That's the first stage.' They all stood rubbing their hands and feeling very happy. 'Now for the bolt,' Pod went on. And the whole performance was repeated; more efficiently, this time—more swiftly. The small bolt, easy in its groove, lifted gently and hung above its socket. 'The window's open,' cried Pod. 'There's nothing holding it now except for the snow on the sill!'

'And we could brush that off—if, say, we went up the ladder,' said Homily. 'And I'd like to see the view.'

'You can see the view in a minute,' said Pod, 'but what we mustn't touch is that snow. You don't want Mabel and Sidney coming upstairs and finding we've been at the window. At least, not yet awhile. . . . What we must do now, and do quickly, is shut it up again. How do you feel, Homily? Like to rest a moment?'

'No, I'm all right,' she said.

'Then we better get going,' said Pod.

CHAPTER SIXTEEN

UNDER POD's direction, and with one or two small mistakes on the parts of Homily and Arrietty, the process was reversed and the latch and bolt made fast again. But not before—as Pod had promised—all three had climbed the ladder in solemn file, and rubbing the misted breath from the glass, had stared out over the landscape. They had seen, so far below them, the dazzling slope of Mr Platter's lawn, the snake-like river, black as a whiplash, curving away into the distance; they had seen the snow-covered roofs of Fordham—and beside a far loop of the stream the three tall poplars, which as they knew marked the site of Little Fordham. They looked very far away—even, thought Homily, as the crow flies. . . .

They did not talk much after they had seen these things.

They felt overawed by the distance, the height and the whiteness. On Pod's orders they set about storing the tackle below the floorboard, where, though safely hidden, it would always be ready to hand. 'We'll practise that window job again tomorrow,' said Pod, 'and every other day from now on.'

As they worked the wind rose again and the underside of the ilex leaves showed grey as the grey sky. Before dusk it began to snow again. When they had set back the board and replaced the nails, they crept up close to the gas-fire and sat there thinking, as the daylight drained from the room. There still seemed no way of escape. 'We're too high,' Homily kept saying. 'Never does and never has done borrowers any good to be high. . . .'

At last the footsteps of Mrs Platter on the stairs drove them back to their box. When the match scraped and the gas-jet flared they saw the room again and the blackness of the window with the snow piled high on the outer sill. The line of white rose softly as they watched it with each descending snowflake.

'Terrible weather,' muttered Mrs Platter to herself, as she set down their plate and their saucer. She stared at them anxiously as they lay huddled in the box and turned up the gas-fire a little before she went away. And they were left as always to eat by themselves in the dark.

CHAPTER SEVENTEEN

THE SNOW and frost and leaden cold continued into early February. Until one morning they woke to soft rain and the pale clouds running in the sky. The leaves of the ilex branch, enamelled and shining, streamed black against the grey and showed no silvery glimpse of underside. 'Wind's in the south,' announced Pod that morning in the satisfied voice of an experienced weather prophet. 'We're likely to have a thaw.'

In the past weeks they had employed their time as best they could. Against the weight of snow on the sill they had practised the raising of the latch and had brought the process to a fine art. Mr and Mrs Platter, they gathered, had been held up on the building of the cage-house, but the borrowers' clothes had arrived, laid out between layers of tissue-paper in a cardboard dress-box. It took them no time at all to get the lid off and with infinite care and cunning to examine the contents and in secret to try them on. The seamstress had nimbler fingers than those of Mrs Platter and had worked in far finer materials. There was a grey suit for Pod with—instead of a shirt—a curious kind of dicky with the collar and tie painted on; there was a pleated and ruched dress for Arrietty with two pinafores to keep it clean. Homily, although ready to grumble, took to her green dress with its 'hint of a bustle', and would wear it sometimes to a moment of danger—the dread sound of footsteps on the stairs.

To Pod these goings-on seemed frivolous and childish. Had they forgotten, he wondered, their immediate danger and the fate which day by day became closer as the weather cleared and Mr Platter worked away on the house? He did not reproach them, however. Let them have their little bit of happiness, he decided, in face of misery to come.

But he became very 'down'. Better they all should be dead, he told them one day, than in lifelong public captivity; and he would sit and stare into space.

He became so 'down' that Homily and Arrietty grew frightened. They stopped dressing up and conferred together in corners. They tried to liven him with little jokes and anecdotes; they saved him all the titbits from the food. But Pod seemed to have lost his appetite. Even when they reminded him that spring was in the air and soon it would be March—'and something always happens to us in

March'—he evinced no interest. 'Something *will* happen to us in March,' was all he said before retreating again into silence.

One day Arrietty came beside him as he sat there, dully thinking, in the corner of the box. She took his hand. 'I have an idea,' she said.

He made an effort to smile and gently squeezed her hand. 'There isn't anything,' he said; 'we've got to face it, lass.'

'But there is something,' Arrietty persisted. 'Do listen, Papa. I've thought of the very thing!'

'Have you, my girl?' he said gently, and, smiling a little, he stroked back the hair from her cheek.

'Yes,' said Arrietty, 'we could make a balloon.'

'A what?' he exclaimed. And Homily, who had been toasting up a sliver of bacon at the gas-fire, came across to them, drawn by the sharpness of his tone.

'We needn't even make it!' Arrietty hurried on. 'There are heaps of balloons in those boxes and we have all those strawberry baskets, and there are diagrams and everything. . . .' She pulled his hand. 'Come and look at this copy of the *Illustrated London News*.'

There was a three-page spread in the *Illustrated London News*—with diagrams, photographs and an expert article, set out comprehensively in columns, on the lately revived sport of free ballooning.

Pod could count and add up, but he could not read, so Arrietty, walking about on the page, read the article aloud. He listened attentively, trying to take it in. 'Let's have that again, lass,' he would say, frowning with his effort to understand.

'Well, move, Mother—please,' Arrietty would say,

because Homily, weak from standing, had suddenly sat down on the page. 'You're on the piece about wind velocity. . . .'

Homily kept muttering phrases like: 'Oh, my goodness—oh, my goodness gracious me . . .' as the full implications of their plan began to dawn on her. She looked strained and a little wild, but awake now to their desperate plight, was resigned to a lesser evil.

'I've got that,' Pod would say at last, after several repetitions of a paragraph concerning something described as 'the canopy or envelope'. 'Now let's have that bit about the valve line and the load ring. It's up near the top of the second column.' And he and Arrietty would walk up the page again and patiently, clearly, although stumbling now and again on the big words, Arrietty would read aloud.

In the tool drawer, no longer out of bounds, they had found the stub of a lead pencil. Pod extracted the lead and sharpened it to a fine point, for Arrietty to underline key headings and to make lists.

At last, on the third day of concentrated homework, Pod announced: 'I'm there!'

He was a changed man suddenly; what had once seemed a

ridiculous flight of fancy on the part of Arrietty could now become sober fact, and he was practical enough to see it.

The first job was swiftly to dismantle the shrimping-net. On this, in more senses than one, would hang all their hopes of success. Homily, with a cut-down morsel of fret-saw blade, taken from a box in the tool drawer, was to cut the knots which secured the net to the frame. Pod would then saw up the frame into several portable lengths and take off the bamboo handle.

'That whole shrimping-net's got to disappear', Pod explained, 'as though it had never existed. We can't have them seeing the frame with the netting part cut away. Once it's in pieces, like, we can hide it under the floor.'

It took less time than they had foreseen and as they laid back the floorboard and dropped the nails into place, Pod—who was not often given to philosophizing—said: 'Funny, when you come to think of it, that this old net we were caught in should turn out to be our salvation.'

That night, when they went to bed, they felt tired but a good deal happier. Pod for some time lay awake, thinking another great test lay before them on the morrow. Could the balloon be filled from the gas-jet? There was a real danger in meddling with gas, he realized uneasily; even adult human beings had met with accidents, let alone disobedient children. He had warned Arrietty about gas in the days when they lived at Firbank, and she, good girl, had respected his advice and had understood the peril. He would of course take every precaution: first the window must be opened wide and the cock of the gas-fire shut off, and the fire allowed to cool down until not a spot of red remained. There was plenty of pressure in the gas-jet; even this very evening, when Mrs Platter had first lit it, he remembered how fiercely it had roared; she had always—he had noticed—to turn it a fraction lower. The ascent to the mantel-shelf could be made via the dummy. It was no use worrying, he decided at last, they were bound to have this try-out and to abide by the result. All the same, it was a long time—several hours it seemed—before Pod fell asleep.

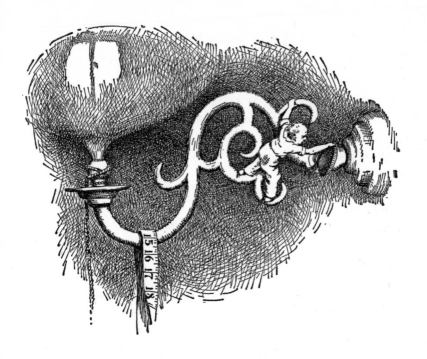

CHAPTER EIGHTEEN

THE BALLOON filled perfectly. Lashed around the nozzle of
the gas-jet and anchored to the horseshoe on the floor by a
separate piece of twine, it first swelled slightly in a limp mass
which hung loosely down against the burner and then—to
their startled joy—suddenly shot upright and went on
swelling. Bigger and bigger it grew—until it became a vast,
tight globe of a rich translucent purple. Then Pod, firmly
perched among the ornate scrollwork of the bracket, leaned
sideways and turned off the gas.

As though making a tourniquet, he tied the neck of the
balloon above the nozzle and undid the lashing just below.
The balloon leapt free almost with a jump but was brought

up short by the tethering string which Pod had anchored
to the horseshoe.

Homily and Arrietty on the floor beside the horseshoe
let out their 'Aaahs' and 'Ohs' . . . and Arrietty ran forward and, seizing the string, tried her weight on it. She
swung a little to and fro as the balloon bumped against the
ceiling.

'Gently!' cried Pod from the bosom of the dummy. He
was climbing down slowly on carefully set footholds of
pins. When he reached the caged part below the dummy's
hips he swung down more quickly from one wire rung to
another.

'Now, we'll all three take hold,' he told them, running to
grasp the string. 'Pull', he cried, 'as hard as you can. Hand
over hand!'

Hand over hand they pulled and swung and slowly the
balloon came down. A swift double turn of the twine
through a nail-hole in the horseshoe and there it was—
tethered beside them, gently swaying and twisting.

Pod wiped his brow on his sleeve. 'It's too small,' he
said.

'Too small!' exclaimed Homily. She felt dwarfed and
awed by the great bobbing purple mass. But it gave her a
feeling of delightful power to push it and make it sway; and
a sideways stroke of her fingers would send it into a spin.

'Of course it's too small,' explained Pod in a worried
voice. 'We shouldn't be able to pull it down like that. A
balloon that size might take Arrietty alone, but it would
not take the three of us—not with the net and the basket
added. And we got to have ballast too.'

'Well,' said Homily, after a short, dismayed silence,
'what are we going to do?'

'I've got to think,' said Pod.

'Suppose we all stopped eating and thinned down a bit?' suggested Homily.

'That wouldn't be any good. And you're thin enough already.' Pod seemed very worried. 'No, I've got to think.'

'There is a bigger balloon,' said Arrietty. 'It's in a box by itself. At least, it looked bigger to me.'

'Well, let's take a look,' said Pod, but he did not sound very hopeful.

It did seem bigger and was covered with shrivelled white markings. 'I think it's some kind of lettering,' Arrietty remarked, turning over the box-lid. 'Yes, it says here: "Printed to your own specification"—I wonder what it means. . . .'

'I don't care what it means,' exclaimed Pod, 'so long as there's room for a lot of it. Yes, it's bigger,' he went on, 'a good deal bigger, and it's heavier. Yes, this balloon may just do us nicely. Might as well try it at once, now we've got the fire off and the window open.'

'What shall we do with this one?' asked Homily from the floor. She tapped it sharply so that it trembled and spun.

'We better burst it,' said Pod on his way down from the table via the raffia ladder which swung on bent pins from the chair back, 'and hide the remains. Nothing much else that we *can* do.'

He burst it with a pin. The report seemed deafening and the balloon, deflating, jumped about like a mad thing; Homily screamed and ran for safety into the wire cage below the dummy. There was a terrible smell of gas.

'Didn't think it would make such a noise,' said Pod, pin in hand and looking rather startled. 'Never mind, with the window open—the smell will soon wear off.'

The new balloon was more cumbersome to climb with and Pod had to rest awhile on the mantel-shelf before he tackled the gas-jet.

'Like me to come up and help you, Papa?' Arrietty called out from the floor.

'No,' he said, 'I'll be all right in a minute. Just let me get my breath. . . .'

The heavier balloon remained limp for longer; until,

almost as though groaning under the effort, it raised itself upright and slowly began to fill. 'Oh,' breathed Arrietty, 'it's going to be a lovely colour. . . .' It was a deep fuchsia pink, becoming each moment—as the rubber swelled—more delicately pale. As it swayed a little on the gas-jet white lettering began to appear. STOP! was the first word, with an exclamation mark after it. Arrietty, reading the word aloud, hoped it was not an omen. Below STOP came the word BALLYHOGGIN, and below that again in slightly smaller print: 'World Famous Model Village and Riverside Teas.'

The balloon was growing larger and larger. Homily looked alarmed. 'Careful, Pod,' she begged; 'whatever you do, don't burst it!'

'It can go a bit more yet,' said Pod. They watched anxiously until at last Pod, in a glow of pink shadow from the swaying monster above him, said: 'That's about it,' and leaning sideways to the wall, sharply turned off the gas. Climbing back, he took up the tape-measure which still hung from the gas-bracket and measured the height of the letter 'i' in 'Riverside Teas'. 'A good three inches,' he said, 'that gives us something to check by the next time we inflate.' He now spoke more often in current ballooning terms and had acquired quite a fair-sized vocabulary concerning such things as flying ballast, rip lines, trail ropes or grapnel hooks.

This time the balloon, soaring to the ceiling, half lifted the horseshoe and dragged it along the floor. With great presence of mind Homily sat down on the horseshoe while Arrietty leapt for the string.

'That looks more like it,' said Pod as he climbed once again down the bosom of the dummy. As he started down excitedly his foot slipped on a pin, but leaning sideways he pushed the pin back in again almost to the head and made the foothold secure. But for the rest of the climb he controlled his eagerness and took the stages more slowly. By the time he reached the floor, in spite of the cold air from the window, he looked very hot and dishevelled.

'Any give on the line?' he asked Arrietty as he waited to recover his breath.

'No,' gasped Arrietty. Then they all three pulled together but the balloon merely twisted on the ceiling as though held there by a magnet.

'That's enough,' said Pod, after they had all three lifted their feet from the floor and had swung about awhile, still with no effect on the balloon. 'Let her go. I've got to think again.'

They were quiet while he did so, but watched anxiously as he paced about frowning with concentration. Once he untethered the balloon from the horseshoe and, tow-line in hand, walked it about on the ceiling. It bumped a little but followed him obediently as he sketched out its course from the floor.

'Time's getting on, Pod,' Homily said at last.

'I know,' he said.

'I mean,' Homily went on in a worried voice. 'How are we going to get it down? I'm thinking of Mabel and Sidney. We've got to get it down before supper, Pod.'

'I know that,' he said. He walked the balloon across the room until he stood below the lip of the table. 'What we need is some kind of winch—some kind of worm and worm-wheel.' He stared up at the knob of the tool-drawer.

'Worm and worm-wheel . . .' said Homily in a mystified voice. '*Worm?*' she repeated incredulously.

Arrietty, up to date now with almost every aspect of free ballooning, including the use of winches, laughed and said: 'It's a thing that takes the weight—supposing, say, you were turning a handle. Like the——' she stopped abruptly, struck by a sudden thought. 'Papa!' she called out excitedly, 'what about the musical-box?'

'The musical-box?' he repeated blankly. Then, as Arrietty nodded, a light dawned and his whole expression changed. 'That's it!' he exclaimed. 'You've hit it. That's our winch-handle, weight, cylinder, worm and wheel and all!'

CHAPTER NINETEEN

IN NO time at all they had the musical box open and Pod, standing on an upturned match-box, was staring down at the works. 'We've got a problem,' he said, as they scrambled up beside him. 'I'll solve it, mind, but I've got to find the right tool. It's those teeth,' he pointed out.

Gazing into the works, they saw he meant a row of metal points suspended downwards from a bar, these were the strikers which, brushing the cylinder as it turned, rang from each prickle one tinkling note of the tune. 'You've got to have those teeth out, or they'd mess up the tow-line. If they're welded in it's going to be difficult, but looks to me as though they're all in a piece held in by those screws.'

'It looks to me like that too,' said Arrietty, leaning forward to see better.

'Well, we'll soon have those screws out,' said Pod.

While he climbed once again to the tool drawer, Homily and Arrietty played one last tune. 'Pity we never heard the others,' said Arrietty, 'and we never shall hear them now.'

'If we get out of here alive', said Homily, 'I don't care if I never see or hear any kind of musical box again in the whole of the rest of my life!'

'Well, you are going to get out of here alive,' remarked Pod in a grimly determined voice. He had come back amongst them with the smallest screwdriver he could find; even then it was as tall as himself. He walked out on the bar and, feet apart, holding the handle at chest level, took his position above the screw and set the edge into the slot.

After a short resistance the screw turned easily as Pod revolved the handle. 'Light as watch screws,' he remarked as he loosened the others. 'It's well made, this musical-box.'

Soon they could lift out the row of spiked teeth and make fast the tow-line to the cylinder. It swayed loosely as the balloon above it surged against the ceiling. 'Now', said Pod, 'I'll take the first turn and we'll see how it goes. . . .'

Arrietty and Homily held their breaths as he grasped the handle of the musical-box and slowly began to turn. The line tautened and became dead straight. Slowly and steadily, as Pod put more effort into his turning, the balloon started down towards them. They watched it anxiously, with upturned faces and aching necks, until at last—swaying and pulling slightly at its moorings—it was brought within their reach.

'What about that?' said Pod in a satisfied voice. But he looked very white and tired.

'What do we do now?' asked Homily.

'We deflate it,' he said.

'Let the gas out,' explained Arrietty as Homily still looked blank.

'We've to find some kind of a platform', announced Pod, 'to set across the top of this musical-box, something we can walk about on. . . .' He looked about the room. Under the gas-ring, on which stood the empty glue-pot, was a small oblong of scorched tin, used to protect the boards of the floor. 'That'll do us,' said Pod.

All three were very tired by now, but they managed to slide the strip of tin from below the gas-ring and hoist it across the opened top of the musical-box. From this platform Pod could handle the neck of the balloon and begin to untie the knot. 'You and Arrietty keep your distance,' he

advised Homily. 'Better go under the table. No knowing what this balloon might do.'

What it did, when released from the knotted twine, was to sail off sideways into the air and, descending slowly, to bump along the floor. With each bump the smell of gas became stronger. It seemed to Arrietty, as she watched it from

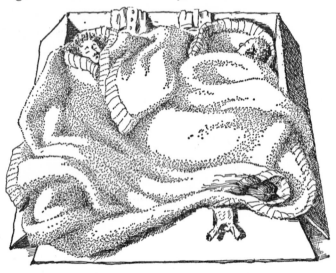

under the table, that the balloon was dying in jerks. At last the envelope lay still and empty and Arrietty and Homily emerged from under the table and stood looking down at it with Pod.

'What a day!' said Homily. 'And we've still got to close the window. . . .'

'It's been a worth-while day,' said Pod.

But by the time they had gone through the elaborate process of closing up the window and had hidden all traces of the recent experiment below the floorboard, they were utterly worn out. It was not yet dusk before they crept wearily into their blanket-lined box and stretched their aching limbs.

By the time Mr and Mrs Platter brought their supper all three were lost to the world in a deep, exhausted sleep. They did not hear Mrs Platter exclaim because the fire was out. Nor did they see Mr Platter sniffing delicately and peering about the room, and complaining that 'You ought to be more careful, Mabel—there's a wicked smell of gas.'

Mrs Platter, very indignant, protested her innocence. 'It was you who lit the gas-fire this morning, Sidney.'

'No, that was yesterday,' he said. And as each knew the other (when caught out in misdoing) to have little regard for truth, they disbelieved each other and came to no conclusion.

'Anyhow', Mrs Platter summed up at last, 'the weather's too mild now for gas-fires. . . .' And they never lit it again.

CHAPTER TWENTY

THE NEXT ten days were confined to serious experiment, controlled and directed by Pod. 'We want to go at it steady now,' he explained. 'Keep to a programme, like, and not try too much at a time. It's a big undertaking, Homily—you don't want to rush it. "Step by step climbs the hill"!'

'But when do they open, Pod?'

'Riverside Teas? April the first, if the cage-house is finished.'

'I'll wager it's finished now. And we're getting well into March. . . .'

'You're wrong, Homily. They've not delivered the plate-glass, nor the handle to lift it up with. And something went wrong with the drainage. They had a flood, remember? Didn't you listen when they were talking?'

'Not if they're talking about the cage-house I don't listen,' said Homily. 'It gives me the creeps to hear them. Once they start on about the cage-house, I go right under the blanket.'

During these busy ten days Pod and Arrietty walked about so much on the open pages of the *Illustrated London News* that the print became quite blurred. They had to discard the idea of a valve at the top of the canopy, to be controlled from below by a line which passed through the open neck into the basket because, as Pod explained to Arrietty, of the nature of the canopy. He touched the diagram with his foot. 'With this kind of fabric balloon you *can* have the valve line through the neck . . . but rubber's like elastic, squeezes the gas out . . . we'd all be gassed in less than ten minutes if we left the neck open like they do.'

He was disappointed about this because he had already invented a way to insert a control valve where it should be—in the top of the canopy, and had practised on the smaller balloons, of which they had an endless supply.

In the meantime, as Homily with a needle ground down by Pod worked on the shaping of the net, he and Arrietty studied 'equilibrium and weight disposal'. A series of loops was made in the tow-line on which, once the balloon was inflated, they would hang up various objects—a strawberry basket, the half-shaped net, a couple of keys, a hollow curtain ring, a tear-off roll of one-and-sixpenny entrance tickets to Ballyhoggin, and lastly they would swing on the line themselves. There came a day when they achieved a perfect balance. Half a dozen one-and-sixpenny entrance tickets, torn off by Arrietty, would raise the balloon two feet; and one small luggage key, hooked on by Pod, would bring it down with a bump.

Still, they could find no way of controlling the gas through the neck. They could go up, but not down. Untying what he called 'the guard knot' at the neck—or even loosening the guard knot—would, Pod thought, be a little too risky. The gas might rush out in a burst (as they had seen it do so often by now) and the whole contraption—balloon, basket, ballast and aeronauts—would drop like a stone to the earth. 'We can't risk that, you know,' Pod said to Arrietty. 'What we need is some sort of valve or lever. . . . ' and for the tenth time that day he climbed back into the tool-drawer.

Arrietty joined Homily in her corner by the box to help her with the load-ring. The net was shaping up nicely and Homily, instructed by Pod and Arrietty, had threaded in and made secure the piece of slightly heavier cord which, as

it encircled the balloon round its fullest circumference, was
suitably called 'the equator'. She was now attaching the
load-ring which, when the balloon was netted, would
encircle the neck and from which they would hang the
basket. They had used the hollow curtain ring, whose
weight was now known and tested. 'It's lovely, Mamma!
You are clever. . . .'

'It's easy,' said Homily, 'once you've got the hang of it.
It's no harder than tatting.'

'You've shaped it so beautifully.'

'Well, your father did the calculations. . . .'

'I've got it!' cried Pod from the tool-drawer. He had
been very quiet for a very long while and now emerged
slowly with a long cylindrical object almost as tall as himself, which he carefully stowed on the table. 'Or so I
believe,' he added, as he climbed up after it by means of the
repair kit. In his hand was a small length of fretsaw blade.

Arrietty ran excitedly across the room and swiftly climbed
up to join him. The long object turned out to be a topless
fountain-pen, with an ink-encrusted nib, one prong of
which was broken. Pod had already unscrewed the pen and
taken it apart, and the nib end now lay on the table attached
to its worm-like rubber tube, with the empty shaft beside it.

'I cut the shaft off here,' said Pod, 'about an inch and a
half from the top, just above the filling lever; then I'll cut off
the closed end of this inner tube—but right at the end, like—
so it sticks out a good inch and a half beyond the cut-off end
of the pen casing. May be more. Now'—he went on, speaking cheerfully but rather ponderously, as though giving a
lesson (a 'do-it-yourself' lesson, thought Arrietty, remem-
bering the Household Hints section in her Diary and
Proverb Book)—'we screw the whole thing together again.

and what do we get? We get a capless fountain-pen with the top of its shaft cut off and an extra bit of tube. Do you follow me?'

'So far,' said Arrietty.

'Then', said Pod, 'we unscrew the nib. . . .'

'Can you?' asked Arrietty.

'Of course,' said Pod; 'they're always changing nibs. I'll show you.' He took up the pen and, straddling the shaft, he gripped it firmly between his legs, and taking the nib in both hands, he quickly unscrewed it at chest level. 'Now', he said as he laid the nib aside, 'we have a circular hole where that nib was—leading straight into the rubber tube. Take a look. . . .'

Arrietty peered down the shaft. 'Yes,' she said.

'Well, there you are,' said Pod.

But where? Arrietty wanted to say; instead she said, more politely: 'I don't think I quite . . .'

'Well,' said Pod in a patient voice as though slightly dashed by her slowness, 'we insert the nib end into the neck of the balloon—after inflation of course, and just below the guard knot. We whip it around with a good firm lashing of twine. I take hold of the filling lever and pull it down sideways at right angles to the pen shaft. That's the working position, with the gas safely shut off. We then untie the guard knot. And there we are: with the cut-off pen shaft and rubber tube hanging down into the basket.' He paused. 'Are you with me? Never mind,' he went on confidently, 'you'll see it as I do it. Now'—he drew a long satisfied breath—'standing in the basket, I reach up my hand to the filling lever and I close it down slowly towards the shaft and the gas flows out through the tube. Feel,' he went on happily, 'the lever's quite loose,' and with one foot on the pen to steady it, he worked the filling lever gently up and down. Arrietty tried it, too. Worn with use, it slid easily.

'Then', said Pod, 'I raise the lever back up so it stands out again at right angles—and the gas is now shut off.'

'It's wonderful,' said Arrietty, but suddenly she thought of something. 'What about all that gas coming down straight into the basket?'

'We leave it behind!' cried Pod. 'Don't you see, girl— the gas is rising all the time and rising faster than the balloon's descending? I thought of that: that's why I wanted that bit of extra tube; we can turn that tube-end upwards, sideways—where we like; but whichever way we turn it the gas'll be rushing upwards and we'll be dropping away from it. See what I mean? Come to think of it, we could bend the tube upwards to start with and clip it to the shaft of the pen. No reason why not.'

He was silent a moment, thinking this over.

'And there won't be all that much gas—not once I've sorted out the lever. You only let it out by degrees. . . .'

During the next few days, which were very exciting, Arrietty often thought of Spiller—how deft he would have been at adjusting the net as the envelope filled at the gas-jet. This was Homily's and Arrietty's job—tiresome pullings by hand or with bone crochet hook, while Pod controlled the intake of gas; the netted canopy would slowly swell above them until the letter 'I' in RIVERSIDE TEAS had achieved its right proportion. The 'equator' of the net, as Pod told them, must bisect the envelope exactly for the load-ring to hang straight and keep the basket level.

Arrietty wished Spiller could have seen the first attachment of the basket by raffia bridles to the load-ring. This took place on the platform of the musical-box, with the basket at this stage weighted down with keys.

And on that first free flight up to the ceiling when Pod, all his attention on the fountain-pen lever, had brought them down so gently, Spiller—Arrietty knew—would have prevented Homily from making the fatal mistake of jumping out of the basket as soon as it touched the floor. At terrifying speed, Pod and Arrietty had shot aloft again, hitting the ceiling with a force which nearly threw them out of the basket, while Homily — in tears—wrung her hands below them. It took a long time to descend, even with the valve wide open, and Pod was very shaken.

'You must remember, Homily,' he told her gravely when, anchored once more to the musical-box, the balloon was slowly deflating, 'you weigh as much as a couple of Gladstone-bag keys and a roll and a half of tickets. No passenger must ever attempt to leave the car or basket until the envelope is completely collapsed.' He looked very serious. 'We were lucky to have a ceiling. Suppose we'd been out of doors—do you know what would have happened?'

'No,' whispered Homily huskily, drying her cheeks with the back of her trembling hand and giving a final sniff.

'Arrietty and me would've shot up to twenty thousand feet and that would have been the end of us. . . .'

'Oh dear. . . .' muttered Homily.

'At that great height', said Pod, 'the gas would expand so quickly that it would burst the canopy.' He stared at her accusingly. 'Unless, of course, we'd had the presence of mind to open the valve and keep it open on the whole rush up. Even then, when we did begin to descend, we'd descend too quickly. We'd have to throw everything overboard— ballast, equipment, clothes, food, perhaps even one of the passengers——'

'Oh no!' gasped Homily.

'And in spite of all this,' Pod concluded, 'we'd probably crash just the same!'

Homily remained silent, and after watching her face for a moment, Pod said more gently:

'This isn't a joy-ride, Homily.'

'I know that,' she retorted with feeling.

CHAPTER TWENTY-ONE

But it did seem a joy-ride to Arrietty when—on 28th March, having opened the window for the last time and left it open, they drifted slowly out into the pale spring sunshine.

The moment of actual departure had come with a shock of surprise, depending as it did on wind and weather. The night before they had gone to bed as usual, and this morning, before Mabel and Sidney had brought their breakfast, Pod, studying the ilex branch, had announced that this was The Day.

It had seemed quite unreal to Arrietty and it still seemed unreal to her now. Their passage was so dreamlike and silent. . . . At one moment they were in the room, which seemed now almost to smell of their captivity, and the next moment—free as thistledown—they sailed softly into a vast ocean of landscape, undulating into distance and brushed with the green veil of spring.

There was a smell of sweet damp earth and for a moment the smell of something frying in Mrs Platter's kitchen. There were myriad tiny sounds—a bicycle bell, the sound of a horse's hoofs and a man's voice growling 'Giddup. . . .' Then suddenly they heard Mrs Platter calling to Mr Platter from a window: 'Put on your coat, dear, if you're going to stay out long. . . .' And, looking down at the gravel path below them, they saw Mr Platter, tool-bag in hand, on his way to the island. He looked a strange shape from above—head down between his shoulders and feet twinkling in and out as he hurried towards his objective.

'He's going to work on the cage-house,' said Homily.

They saw with a kind of distant curiosity the whole layout of Mr Platter's model village, and the river twisting away beyond it to the three distant poplars which marked what Pod now referred to as their L.Z.[1]

During the last few days he had taken to using abbreviations of ballooning terms, referring to the musical-box as the T.O.P.[2] They were now, with the gleaming slates of roof just below them, feeling their way towards a convenient C.A.[3]

Strangely enough, after their many trial trips up and down from the ceiling, the basket felt quite home-like and familiar. Arrietty, whose job was 'ballast', glanced at her father, who stood looking rapt and interested—but not too preoccupied—with his hand on the lever of the cut-off fountain-pen. Homily, although a little pale, was matter-of-factly adjusting the coiled line of the grapnel, one spike of which had slid below the level of the basket. 'Might just catch in something,' she murmured. The grapnel consisted of two large open safety-pins, securely wired back to back. Pod, who for days had been studying the trend of the ilex leaves, remarked: 'Wind's all right but not enough of it. . . .' as very gently, as though waltzing, they twisted above the roof. Pod, looking ahead, had his eye on the ilex.

'A couple of tickets now, Arrietty,' he said; 'takes a few minutes to feel the effect. . . .'

She tore them off and dropped them overboard. They fluttered gently and ran a little on the slates on the roof and then lay still.

'Let's give her two more,' said Pod. And within a few

[1] Landing Zone.   [2] Take off Point.
        [3] Chosen Altitude.

seconds, staring at the ilex-tree as slowly it loomed nearer, he added: 'Better make it three. . . .'

'We've had six shillings' worth already,' Arrietty protested.

'All right,' said Pod, as the balloon began to lift, 'let's leave it at that.'

'But I've done it now,' she said.

They sailed over the ilex-tree with plenty of height to spare and the balloon still went on rising. Homily gazed down as the ground receded.

'Careful, Pod,' she said.

'It's all right,' he told them, 'I'm bringing her down.' And in spite of the upturned tube they smelled a slight smell of gas.

Even from this height the noises were quite distinct. They heard Mr Platter hammering at the cage-house and, although the railway looked so distant, the sound of a shunting train. As they swept down rather faster than Pod had bargained for, they found themselves carried beyond the confines of Mr Platter's garden and drifting—on a descending spiral—above the main road. A farm cart crawled slowly beneath them on the broad sunlit stretch which, curving ribbon-like into the distance, looked frayed along one side by the shadows thrown from the hedges and from the spindly wayside woods. There was a woman on the shafts of the farm cart and a man asleep in the back.

'We're heading away from our L.Z.' said Pod. 'Better give her three more tickets—there's less wind down here than above. . . .'

As the balloon began to lift they passed over one of Mr Platter's lately built villas in which someone was practising the piano—a stream of metallic notes flowed up and about them. And a dog began to bark.

They began to rise quite swiftly—on the three legitimate tickets—and an extra one-and-sixpennyworth thrown down by Arrietty. She did it on an impulse and knew at once that it was wrong. Their very lives depended on obedience to the pilot, and how could the pilot navigate if she cheated on commands? She felt very guilty as the balloon continued to rise. They were passing over a field of cows which, second by second, as she stared down at them, were becoming steadily smaller; all the same, a tremulous 'Moo' surged up to them through the quiet air and eddied about their ears. She could hear a lark singing—and over a spreading cherry orchard she smelled the sticky scent of sun-warmed buds and blossoms. 'It's more like mid April', Arrietty thought, 'than the 28th of March.'

'Spiller would have liked this,' she said aloud.

'Maybe,' said Homily rather grimly.

'When I grow up I think I'll marry Spiller . . .'

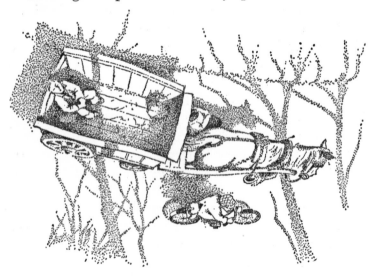

'Spiller!' exclaimed Homily in an astounded voice.

'What's wrong with him?' asked Arrietty.

'There's nothing exactly wrong with him,' admitted Homily grudgingly. 'I mean if you tidied him up a bit. . . . But where do you imagine you'd live? He's always on the move.'

'I'd be on the move too,' said Arrietty.

Homily stared at her. 'Whatever will you think of to say next? And what a place to choose to say it in. Marry Spiller! Did you hear that, Pod?'

'Yes, I heard,' he said.

The balloon was still rising.

'He likes the out-of-doors, you see,' said Arrietty, 'and I like it, too.'

'Marry *Spiller*. . . .' Homily repeated to herself—she could not get over it.

'And if we were always on the move, we'd be freer to come and see you more often . . .'

'So it's got to "we"!' said Homily.

'. . . and I couldn't do that', Arrietty went on, 'if I married into a family with a set house the other side of Bedfordshire——'

'But you're only sixteen!' exclaimed Homily.

'Seventeen—nearly,' said Arrietty. She was silent a moment and then she said, 'I think I ought to tell him——'

'Pod!' exclaimed Homily, 'do you hear? It must be the height or something, but this child's gone out of her senses!'

'I'm trying to find the wind,' said Pod, staring steadily upwards to where a slight film of mist appeared to drift towards the sun.

'You see,' Arrietty went on quietly (she had been thinking

of her talks with Miss Menzies and of those blue eyes full of tears), 'he's so shy and he goes about so much, he might never think of asking me. And one day he might get tired of being lonely and marry some'—Arrietty hesitated—'some *terribly nice* kind of borrower with very fat legs. . . .'

'There isn't such a thing as a borrower with fat legs,' exclaimed Homily, 'except perhaps your Aunt Lupy. Not that I've actually ever seen her legs. . . .' she added thoughtfully, gazing upwards as though following the direction of Pod's eyes. Then she snapped back again to the subject. 'What nonsense you do talk, Arrietty,' she said. 'I can't imagine what sort of rubbish you must have been reading in that *Illustrated London News*. Why, you and Spiller are more like brother and sister!'

Arrietty was just about going to say—but she couldn't quite find the words—that this seemed quite a good kind of trial run for what was after all a lifelong companionship, when something came between them and the sun and a sudden chill struck the basket. The top of the envelope had melted into mist and the earth below them disappeared from sight.

They stared at each other. Nothing else existed now except the familiar juice-stained basket, hung in a limbo of whiteness, and their three rather frightened selves.

'It's all right,' said Pod, 'we're in a cloud. I'll let out a little gas. . . .'

They were silent while he did so, staring intently at his steady hand on the lever—it hardly seemed to move.

'Not too much,' he explained in a quiet conversational voice. 'The condensation on the net will help us: there's a lot of weight in water. And I think we've found the wind!'

CHAPTER TWENTY-TWO

THEY WERE in sunshine again quite suddenly and cruising smoothly and softly on a gentle breeze towards their still distant L.Z.

'Shouldn't wonder', remarked Pod cheerfully, 'if we hadn't hit on our right C.A. at last.'

Homily shivered. 'I didn't like that at all.'

'Nor did I,' agreed Arrietty. There was no sense of wind in the basket and she turned up her face to the sun, basking gratefully in the suddenly restored warmth.

They passed over a group of cottages set about a small, squat church. Three people with baskets were grouped about a shop, and they heard a sudden peal of very hearty laughter. In a back garden they saw a woman with her back to them, hanging washing on a line; it hung quite limply.

'Not much wind down there,' remarked Pod.

'Nor all that much up here,' retorted Homily.

They stared down in silence for a while.

'I wonder why no one ever looks up,' Arrietty exclaimed suddenly.

'Human beings don't look up much,' said Pod. 'Too full of their own concerns.' He thought a moment. 'Unless, maybe, they hear a sudden loud noise . . . or see a flash or something. They don't have to keep their eyes open like borrowers do.'

'Or birds,' said Arrietty, 'or mice . . .'

'Or anything that's hunted,' said Pod.

'Isn't there anything that hunts human beings?' Arrietty asked.

'Not that I know of,' said Pod. 'Might do 'em a bit of good if there were. Show 'em what it feels like, for once.' He was silent a moment and then said: 'Some say they hunt each other——'

'Oh no!' exclaimed Homily, shocked. (Strictly brought up in the borrowers' code of one-for-all and all-for-one, it was as though he had accused the human race of cannibalism.) 'You shouldn't say such things, Pod—no kind of creature could be as bad as that!'

'I've heard it said!' he persisted stolidly. 'Sometimes singly and sometimes one lot against another lot!'

'All of them human beings?' Homily exclaimed incredulously.

Pod nodded. 'Yes,' he said, 'all of them human beings.'

Horrified but fascinated, Homily stared down below at a man on a bicycle, as though unable to grasp such depravity. He looked quite ordinary—almost like a borrower from here—and wobbled slightly on the lower slopes of what appeared to be a hill. She stared incredulously until the rider turned into the lower gate of the churchyard.

There was a sudden smell of Irish stew, followed by a whiff of coffee.

'Must be getting on for midday,' said Pod, and as he spoke the church clock struck twelve.

'I don't like these eddies,' said Pod some time later, as the balloon once again on a downward spiral curved away from the river; 'something to do with the ground warming up and that bit of hill over there.'

'Would anybody like something to eat?' suggested Homily suddenly. There were slivers of ham, a crumbly knob of cheese, a few grains of cold rice pudding and a long segment of orange on which to quench their thirst.

'Better wait awhile,' said Pod, his hand on the valve. The balloon was moving downwards.

'I don't see why,' said Homily; 'it must be long past one.'

'I know,' said Pod, 'but it's better we hold off, if we can. We may have to jettison the rations, and you can't do that once you've eaten them.'

'I don't know what you mean,' complained Homily.

'Throw the food overboard,' explained Arrietty, who, on Pod's orders, had torn off several more tickets.

'You see,' said Pod, 'what with one thing and another, I've let out a good deal of gas.'

Homily was silent. After a while she said: 'I don't like the way we keep turning round; first the church is on our right, the next it's run round to the left. I mean, you don't know where you are, not for two minutes together.'

'It'll be all right', said Pod, 'once we've hit the wind. Let go another two,' he added to Arrietty.

It was just enough; they rose gently and, held on a steady current, moved slowly towards the stream.

'Now,' said Pod, 'if we keep on this, we're all right.' He stared ahead to where, speckled by the sunshine, the poplar-trees loomed nearer. 'We're going nicely now.'

'You mean we might hit Little Fordham?'

'Not unlikely,' said Pod.

'If you ask me,' exclaimed Homily, screwing up her eyes against the afternoon sun, 'the whole thing's hit or miss!'

'Not altogether,' said Pod, and he let out a little more gas. 'We bring her down slowly, gradually losing altitude. Once we're in reach of the ground we steady her with the trail rope. Acts like a kind of brake. And directly I give her the word, Arrietty releases the grapnel.'

Homily was silent again. Impressed, but still rather anxious, she stared steadily ahead. The river swam gently towards them until and at last it came directly below. The light wind seemed to follow the river's course as it curved ahead into distance. The poplars now seemed to beckon as they swayed and stirred in the breeze, and their long shadows—even longer by now—were stretching directly towards them. They sailed as though drawn on a string.

Pod let out more gas. 'Better uncoil the trail rope,' he said to Arrietty.

'Already?'

'Yes,' said Pod, 'you got to be prepared. . . .'

The ground swayed slowly up towards them. A clump of oak-trees seemed to move aside and they saw just ahead and slightly tilted a bird's-eye view of their long lost Little Fordham.

'You wouldn't credit it!' breathed Homily as, enraptured, they stared ahead.

They could see the railway lines glinting in the sunshine, the weathercock flashing on the church steeple, the un-even roofs along the narrow High Street and the crooked chimney of their own dear home. They saw the garden front of Mr Pott's thatched cottage, and beyond the dark green of the holly hedge a stretch of sunlit lane. A tweed-clad figure strode along it, in a loose-limbed, youthful way. They knew it was Miss Menzies—going home to tea. And Mr Pott, thought Arrietty, would have gone inside for his.

The balloon was sinking fast.

'Careful, Pod!' urged Homily, 'or you'll have us in the river!'

As swiftly the balloon sank down, a veil-like something suddenly appeared along the edge of the garden. As they swam down they saw it to be a line of strong wire fencing girding the bank of the river. Mr Pott had taken pre-cautions and his treasures were now caged in.

'Time, too!' said Homily grimly. Then suddenly she shrieked and clung to the sides of the basket as the stream rushed up towards them.

'Get ready the grapnel!' shouted Pod. But even as he spoke the basket had hit the water and, tilted sideways in a flurry of spray, they were dragged along the surface. All three were thrown off balance and, knee-deep in rushing water, they clung to raffia bridles while the envelope surged on ahead. Pod just managed to close the valve as Arrietty, clinging on with one hand, tried with the other to free the grapnel. But Homily, in a panic and before anyone could stop her, threw out the knob of cheese. The balloon shot violently upwards, accompanied by Homily's screams, and then—just as violently—snapped back to a sickening halt. The roll of tickets shot up between them and sailed down into the water. Except for their grasp on the bridles the occupants would have followed; they were thrown up into the air, where they hung for a moment before tumbling back into the basket: a safety-pin of the grapnel had caught in the wire of the fence. The trembling, creakings, twistings and strainings seemed enough to uproot the fence, and Pod, looking downwards as he clung to the reopened valve lever, saw the barb of the safety-pin slide.

'That won't hold for long,' he gasped.

The quivering basket was held at a terrifying tilt—almost pulled apart, it seemed, between the force of the upward surge and the drag of the grapnel below. The gas was escaping too slowly—it was clearly a race against time.

There was a steady stream of water from the dripping basket. Their three backs were braced against the tilted

floor and their feet against one side. As, white-faced, they all stared downwards they could hear each other's breathing. The angle of the opened pin was slowly growing wider.

Pod took a sudden resolve. 'Get hold of the trail rope', he said to Arrietty, 'and pass it over to me. I'm going down the grapnel-line and taking the trail rope with me.'

'Oh, Pod!' cried Homily miserably, 'suppose we shot up without you!'

He took no notice. 'Quick!' he urged. And, as Arrietty pulled up the length of dripping twine, he took one end in his hand and swung over the edge of the basket on to the line of the grapnel. He slid away below them in one swift downward run, his elbow encircling the trail rope. They watched him steady himself on the top of the fence and climb down a couple of meshes. They watched his swift one-handed movements as he passed the trail rope through the mesh and made fast with a double turn.

Then his small square face turned up towards them.

'Get a hold on the bridles,' he called, 'there's going to be a bit of a jerk. . . .' He shifted himself a few meshes sideways, from where he could watch the pin.

It slid free with a metallic ping, even sooner than they had expected, and was flung out in a quivering arch which, whiplike, thrashed the air. The balloon shot up in a frenzied leap but was held by the knotted twine. It seemed frustrated as it strained above them, as though striving to tear itself free. Arrietty and Homily clung together, half laughing and half crying, in a wild access of relief. He had moored them just in time.

'You'll be all right now,' Pod called up cheerfully; 'nothing to do but wait,' and after staring a moment reflectively, he began to climb down the fence.

'Where are you going, Pod?' Homily cried out shrilly.

He paused and looked up again. 'Thought I'd take a look at the house—our chimney's smoking, seems like there's someone inside.'

'But what about us?' cried Homily.

'You'll come down slowly, as the envelope deflates, and then you can climb down the fence. I'll be back,' he added.

'Of all the things,' exclaimed Homily, 'to go away and leave us!'

'What do you want me to do?' asked Pod. 'Just stand down below and watch? I won't be long and—say it's Spiller—he's likely to give us a hand. You're all right,' he went on. 'Take a pull on the trail rope as the balloon comes down, that'll bring you alongside.'

'Of all the things!' exclaimed Homily again incredulously, as Pod went on climbing down.

CHAPTER TWENTY-THREE

THE DOOR of Vine Cottage was unlocked and Pod pushed it open. A fire was burning in an unfamiliar grate and Spiller lay asleep on the floor. As Pod entered he scrambled to his feet. They stared at each other. Spiller's pointed face looked tired and his eyes a little sunken.

Pod smiled slowly. 'Hallo,' he said.

'Hallo,' said Spiller, and without any change of expression he stooped and picked some nutshells from the floor and threw them on to the fire. It was a new floor, Pod noticed, of honey-coloured wood, with a woven mat beside the fireplace.

'Been away quite a while,' remarked Spiller casually, staring at the blaze. The changed fireplace, Pod noticed, now incorporated a small iron cooking-stove.

'Yes,' he said, looking about the room, 'we've been all winter in an attic.'

Spiller nodded.

'*You* know,' said Pod, 'a room at the top of a human house.'

Spiller nodded again and kicked a piece of fallen nutshell back into the grate. It flared up brightly with a cheerful crackle.

'We couldn't get out,' said Pod.

'Ah,' said Spiller non-committally.

'So we made a balloon,' went on Pod, 'and we sailed it out of the window.' Spiller looked up sharply, suddenly alert. 'Arrietty and Homily are in it now. It's caught on the wire fence.'

Spiller's puzzled glance darted towards the window and as swiftly darted away again: the fence was not visible from here.

'Some kind of boat?' he said at last.

'In a manner of speaking,' Pod smiled. 'Care to see it?' he added carelessly.

Something flashed in Spiller's face—a spark which was swiftly quenched. 'Might as well,' he conceded.

'May interest you,' said Pod, a note of pride in his voice. He glanced once more about the room.

'They've done the house up,' he remarked.

Spiller nodded. 'Running water and all . . .'

'Running water!' exclaimed Pod.

'That's right,' said Spiller, edging towards the door.

Pod stared at the piping above the sink but he made no move to inspect it. Tables and floor were strewn with Spiller's borrowings: sparrows' eggs and eggshells, nuts, grain and, laid out on a dandelion leaf, six rather shrivelled smoked minnows.

'Been staying here?' he said.

'On and off,' said Spiller, teetering on the threshold.

Again Pod's eyes travelled about the room: the general style of it emerged, in spite of Spiller's clutter—plain chairs, scrubbable tables, wooden dresser, painted plates, hand-woven rugs, all very Rossetti-ish and practical.

'Smells of humans,' he remarked.

'Does a bit,' agreed Spiller.

'We might just tidy round,' Pod suggested, 'wouldn't take us a minute.' As though in apology, he added: 'It's first impressions with her, if you get my meaning. Always has been. And——' he broke off abruptly as a sharp sound split the silence.

'What's that?' said Spiller, as eye met startled eye.

'It's the balloon,' cried Pod, and, suddenly white-faced, he stared in a stunned way at the window. 'They've burst it,' he exclaimed and, pushing past Spiller, he dashed out through the door.

Homily and Arrietty, shaken but unharmed, were clinging to the wires. The basket dangled emptily and the envelope, in tatters, seemed threaded into the fence; the net now looked like a bird's nest.

'We got it down lovely,' Pod heard Homily gasping, as hand over hand, he and Spiller climbed up the mesh of the fence.

'Stay where you are,' Pod called out.

'Came down like a dream, Pod,' Homily kept on crying. 'Came down like a bird. . . .'

'All right,' called Pod, 'just you stay quiet where you are.'

'Then the wind changed', persisted Homily, half sobbing but still at the top of her voice, 'and swung us round sideways . . . against that jagged wire. . . . But she came down lovely, Pod, light as thistledown. Didn't she, Arrietty?'

But Arrietty, too proud to be rescued, was well on her way to the ground. Spiller climbed swiftly towards her and they met in a circle of mesh. 'You're on the wrong side,' said Spiller.

'I know, I can soon climb through.' There were tears in her eyes, her cheeks were crimson and her hair blew about in wisps.

'Like a hand?' said Spiller.

'No, thank you. I'm quite all right,' and avoiding his

curious gaze, she hurriedly went on down. 'How stupid, how stupid,' she exclaimed aloud when she felt herself out of earshot. She was almost in tears: it should never have been like this: he would never understand the balloon without having seen it inflated, and mere words could never make clear all they had gone through to make it and the extent of their dizzy success. There was nothing to show for

this now but a stained old strawberry basket, some shreds of shrivelled rubber and a tangled bunch of string. A few moments earlier she and her mother had been bringing it down so beautifully. After the first flurry of panic Homily had had one of her sudden calms. Perhaps it was the realiza- tion of being home again; the sight of their unchanged village at peace in the afternoon light; and the filament of smoke which rose up unexpectedly from the chimney of Vine Cottage, a drifting pennant of welcome which showed the house was inhabited and that the fire had only just been lit. Not lit by Miss Menzies, who had long since passed out of sight; nor Pod, who had not yet reached the house, so they guessed it must be Spiller. They had suddenly felt among friends again and, proud of their great achievement, they had longed to show off their prowess. In a business-like manner they had coiled up the ropes, stacked the tackle and made the basket shipshape. They had wrung out their wet clothes and Homily had redone her hair. Then, methodically and calmly, they had set to work, following Pod's instructions.

'It's too bad,' Arrietty exclaimed, looking upwards, as she reached the last rung of the wire: there was her father helping Homily with footholds, and Spiller of course at the top of the fence busily engaged in examining the wreckage. Very dispirited, she stepped off the wire, drew down a plantain leaf by it's tip, and flinging herself along it's springy length she lay there glumly, staring upwards, her hands behind her head.

Homily too seemed very upset when, steered by Pod, she eventually reached the ground. 'It was nothing we did,' she kept saying, 'it was just a change of wind.'

'I know, I know,' he consoled her; 'forget it now—it served it's purpose and there's a surprise for you up at the house. You and Arrietty go on ahead while Spiller and I do the salvage. . . .'

When Homily saw the house she became a different creature: it was as though, thought Arrietty, watching her mother's expression, Homily had walked into paradise. There were a few stunned moments of quiet incredulous joy before excitement broke loose and she ran like a mad thing from room to room, exploring, touching, adjusting and endlessly exclaiming. 'They've divided the upstairs into two, there's a little room for you, Arrietty. Look at this sink, I ask you, Arrietty! Water in the tap and all! And what's that thing on the ceiling?'

'It's a bulb from a hand torch of some kind,' said Arrietty, after a moment's study. And beside the backdoor, in a kind of lean-to shed, they found the great square battery.

'So we've got electric light . . .' breathed Homily, slowly backing away, 'better not touch it', she went on, in an awe-struck and frightened voice, 'until your father comes. Now help me clear up Spiller's clobber,' she continued excitedly; 'I pity any unfortunate creature who ever keeps house for *him*. . . .' But her eyes were alight and shining. She hung up her new dress beside the fire to dry and, delighted to find them again, she changed into old clothes. Arrietty, who for some reason still felt dispirited, found she had grown out of hers.

'I look ridiculous in this,' she said unhappily, trying to pull down her jersey.

'Well, who's to see you,' Homily retorted, 'except your father and Spiller?'

Panting and straining, she worked away, clearing and stacking and altering the positions of the furniture. Soon nothing was where it had been originally and the room looked rather odd.

'You can't do *much* with a kitchen–living-room,' Homily remarked when, panting a little, she surveyed the general post, 'and I'm still not sure about that dresser.'

'What about it?' said Arrietty, who was longing to sit down.

'That it wouldn't be better where it was.'

'Can't we leave the men to do it?' said Arrietty. 'They'll be back soon—for supper.'

'That's just the point,' said Homily. 'If we move it at all
we must do it now, before I start on the cooking. It looks
dreadful there,' she went on crossly. 'Spoils the whole look
of the room. Now come on, Arrietty—it won't take us a
minute.'

With the dresser back in its old position the other things
looked out of place. 'Now that table could go here,' Homily
suggested, 'if we move this chest of drawers. You take one
end, Arrietty. . . .'

There were several more reshuffles before she seemed
content. 'A lot of trouble,' she admitted happily, as she
surveyed the final result, 'but worth it in the end. It looks a
lot better now, doesn't it, Arrietty? It suddenly looks kind
of *right*.'

'Yes,' said Arrietty dryly, 'because everything's back
where it was.'

'What do you mean?' exclaimed Homily.

'Where it was before we started,' said Arrietty.

'Nonsense,' snapped Homily crossly, but she looked
about her uncertainly. 'Why—that stool was under the
window! But we can't waste time arguing now: those men
will be back any moment and I haven't started the soup.
Run down to the stream now, there's a good girl, and get
me a few leaves of watercress. . . .'

CHAPTER TWENTY-FOUR

LATER THAT night when—having eaten and cleared away—
the four of them sat round the fire, Arrietty began to feel a
little annoyed with Spiller. Balloon crazy—that's what he
seemed to have become; and all within a few short hours.
No eyes, no ears, nor thoughts for anyone or anything
except for those boring shreds of shrivelled rubber, now
safely stored with the other trappings in the back of the
village shop. He had listened, of course, at supper when
Arrietty, hoping to interest him, had tried to recount their
adventures, but if she paused even for a moment the bright
dark glance would fly again to Pod and again, in his tense,
dry way he would ply Pod with questions: 'Oiled silk
instead of rubber next time for the canopy? The silk would
be easy to borrow—and Mr Pott would have the oil. . . .'
Questions on wind velocity, trail ropes, moorings, grapnels,
inflation—there seemed no end to these nor to his curiosity
which, for some masculine reason Arrietty could not
fathom, could only be satisfied by Pod. Any timid contribu-
tion on the part of Arrietty seemed to slide across his mind
unheard. 'And I know as much about it as anybody,' she told
herself crossly, as she huddled in the shadows. 'More in
fact. It was I who had to teach Papa.' She stared in a bored
way about the firelit room: the drawn curtains, plates
glinting on the dresser, the general air of peace and comfort.
Even this, in a way, they owed entirely to her: it was she
who had had the courage to speak to Miss Menzies—and,
in the course of this friendship, describe their habits and
needs. How cosy they all looked in their ignorance, sitting

smugly around the fire. Leaning forward suddenly, right into the firelight, she said: 'Papa, would you listen, please?'

'Don't see why not,' replied Pod, smiling slightly at the eager, firelit face and the breathless tone of her voice.

'It's something I've got to tell you. I couldn't once. But I can now. . . .' As she spoke her heart began to beat a little faster: even Spiller, she saw, was paying attention. 'It's about this house; it's about why they made these things for us; it's about how they knew what we wanted. . . .'

'What *we* wanted . . . ?' repeated Pod.

'Yes, or why do you think they did it?'

Pod took his time. 'I wouldn't know for *why* they did it', he said at last, 'any more than I'd know for *why* they built that church or the railway. Reckon they're furnishing all these houses . . . one by one, like.'

'No,' exclaimed Arrietty, and her voice trembled slightly, 'you're wrong, Papa. They've only furnished one house and that's our house—because they know all about us and they like us and they want us to stay here!'

There was a short, stunned silence. Then Homily muttered: 'Oh, my goodness . . .' under her breath.

Spiller, still as stone, stared unblinkingly, and Pod said slowly: 'Explain what you mean, Arrietty. How do they know about us?'

'I told her,' said Arrietty.

'Her-r?' repeated Pod slowly, rolling his r-rs in the country way, his custom when deeply moved.

'Miss Menzies,' said Arrietty; 'the tall one with the long hands, who hid behind the thistle.'

'Oh, my goodness . . .' muttered Homily again.

'It's all right, Mother,' Arrietty assured her earnestly.

'There's nothing to be frightened of. You'll be safe here, safer than you've ever been—in the whole of all your life. They'll look after us, and protect us and take care of us—for ever and ever and ever. She promised me.'

Homily, though trembling, looked slightly reassured.

'What does your father think?' she asked faintly, and stared across at Pod. Arrietty too wheeled round towards him. 'Don't say anything, Papa, not yet, please . . . please! Not until I've told you everything, then'—at the sight of his expression she lost her nerve, and finished lamely—'then you're practically sure to see.'

'See what?' said Pod.

'That it's quite all right.'

'Go on, then,' he said.

Hurriedly, almost pleadingly, Arrietty gave them the facts. She described her friendship with Miss Menzies right from the very beginning. She described Miss Menzies's character, her loyalty, her charity, her gifts, her imagination and her courage. She even told them about dear Gadstone and about Aubrey, Miss Menzies's 'best friend' (Homily shook her head there, and clicked her tongue. 'Sad when that happens,' she said musingly. 'It was like that with my younger sister, Milligram; Milli never married neither. She took to col- lecting dead flies' wings, making them into fans and suchlike. And pretty they looked, in certain lights, all colours of the rainbow . . .'), and went on to describe all she had learned from Miss Menzies concerning Mr Pott: how kind he was, and how gentle, and so skilled in making-do and invention that he might be a borrower himself.

'That's right,' Spiller said suddenly at this juncture. He spoke so feelingly that Arrietty, looking across at him, felt something stir in her memory.

'Was *he* the borrower you once told us about—the one you said lived here alone?'

Spiller smiled slyly. 'That's right,' he admitted; 'learn a lot from him, *any* borrower could.'

'Not when everything's laid on', said Pod, 'and there's nothing left to borrow. Go on, Arrietty,' he said, as she suddenly seemed lost in thought.

'Well, that's all. At least all I can think of now.'

'It's enough,' said Pod. He stared across at her, his arms folded, his expression very grave. 'You shouldn't have done it,' he said quietly, 'no matter what it's given us.'

'Listen, Pod,' Homily put in quickly, 'she has done it and she can't undo it now, however much you scold her. I mean'—she glanced about the firelit room, at the winking plates on the dresser, the tap above the sink, the unlit globe in the ceiling—'we've a lot to be thankful for.'

'It all smells of humans,' said Pod.

'That'll wear off, Pod.'

'Will it?' he said.

Arrietty, suddenly out of patience, jumped up from her stool by the fire. 'I just don't know what any of you do want,' she exclaimed unhappily. 'I thought you might be pleased or proud of me or something. Mother's always longed for a house like this!' and fumbling at the latch, she opened the door, and ran out into the moonlight.

There was silence in the room after she had gone. No one moved until a stool squeaked slightly, as Spiller rose to his feet.

'Where are you off to?' asked Pod casually.

'Just to take a look at my moorings.'

'But you'll come back here to sleep?' said Homily; very

hospitable, she felt suddenly, surrounded by new-found
amenities.

'Thanks,' said Spiller.

'I'll come with you,' said Pod.

'No need,' said Spiller.

'I'd like the air,' said Pod.

Arrietty, in the shadow of the house, saw them go by in

the moonlight. As they passed out of sight, into darkness,
she heard her father say: '. . . depends how you look at it.'
Look at what, she wondered? Suddenly Arrietty felt left out
of things: her father and mother had their house, Spiller
had his boat, Miss Menzies had Mr Pott and his village,
Mr Pott had Miss Menzies and his railway, but what was
left for her? She reached out and took hold of a dandelion
stalk the size of a lamp-post which had grown beside the
house to the height of her bedroom window. On a sudden
impulse she snapped the stalk in half: the silver seeds
scattered madly into the moonlight and the juice ran out on

her hands. For a moment she stood there watching until the silky spikes, righting themselves, had floated into darkness, and then, suddenly feeling cold, she turned and went inside.

Homily still sat where they had left her, dreaming by the fire. But she had swept the hearth and lighted a dip, which shed its glow from the table. Arrietty, with a sudden pang, saw her mother's deep content.

'Would you like to live here always?' she asked as she drew up a stool to the fire.

'Yes,' said Homily, 'now we've got it comfortable. Why? Wouldn't you?'

'I don't know,' said Arrietty. 'All those people in the summer. All the dust and noise. . . .'

'Yes,' said Homily, 'you've got to keep on weeping. But there's always something,' she added, 'and at least we've got running water.'

'And being cooped up during visiting hours. . . .'

'I don't mind that,' said Homily; 'there's plenty to do in the house and I've been cooped up all my life. That's your lot, like, say you're born a borrower.'

Arrietty was silent a moment. 'It would never be Spiller's lot,' she said at last.

'Oh, him!' exclaimed Homily impatiently. 'I've never known nothing about those out-of-door ones. A race apart, my father used to say. Or house-borrowers just gone wild. . . .'

'Where have they gone?'

'They're all over the place, I shouldn't wonder, hidden away in the rabbit holes and hedges.'

'I mean my father and Spiller.'

'Oh, them. Down to the stream to see to his moorings. And if I was you, Arrietty,' Homily went on more earnestly,

'I'd get to bed before your father comes in—your bed's all ready, new sheets and everything, *and* '—her voice almost broke with pride—'under the quilt, there's a little silken eiderdown!'

'They're coming now,' said Arrietty. 'I can hear them.'

'Well, just say good night and run off,' urged Homily anxiously. As the latch clicked she dropped her voice to a whisper: 'I think you've upset him a bit with that talk about Miss—Miss——'

'Menzies,' said Arrietty.

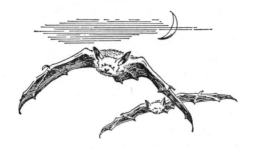

CHAPTER TWENTY-FIVE

THERE WAS a strange aura about Pod when he entered the room with Spiller: it was more than a night-breath of leaves and grasses and a moon-cold tang of water; it was a strength and a stillness, Arrietty thought when she went to kiss him good night, but he seemed very far away. He received her kiss without a word and mechanically pecked at her ear but, as she went off towards the stairs, he suddenly called her back.

'Just a minute, Arrietty. Sit down, Spiller,' he said. He drew up a chair and once more they encircled the fire.

'What's the matter, Pod?' asked Homily. She put out a nervous arm and drew Arrietty closer beside her. 'Is it something you've seen?'

'I haven't seen nothing,' said Pod, 'only moon on the water, a couple of bats and this telltale smoke from our chimney.

'Then let the child go to bed, it's been a long day.'

'I been thinking,' said Pod.

'It seems more like two days,' Homily went on, 'I mean, now you begin to look back on it.' And suddenly, incredibly, it seemed to her, that on this very morning they had wakened still as prisoners and here they were—home again and united about a hearth! Not the same hearth, a better hearth and a home beyond their dreams. 'You take the dip now,' she said to Arrietty, 'and get yourself into bed. Spiller can sleep down here. Take a drop of water up if you like to have a wash: there's plenty in the tap——'

'It won't do,' said Pod suddenly.

They all turned and looked at him. 'What won't do?' faltered Homily.

Pod waved an arm. 'All this. None of it will do. Not one bit of it. And Spiller agrees with me.'

Arrietty's glance flew across to Spiller: she noticed the closed look, the set gleam and the curt, unsmiling nod.

'What could you be meaning, Pod?' Homily moistened her lips. 'You couldn't be meaning this house?'

'That's just what I do mean,' said Pod.

'But you haven't really seen it, Pod,' Homily protested. 'You've never tried the switch, yet. Nor the tap either. You haven't even seen upstairs. You should see what they've done at the top of the landing, how Arrietty's room opens out of ours, like——'

'Wouldn't make no difference,' said Pod.

'But you liked it here, Pod,' Homily reminded him, 'before that attic lot took us away. You was whistling again and singing as you worked, like you did in the old days at Firbank. Wasn't he, Arrietty?'

'I didn't know then', said Pod, 'the thing that we all know now—that these humans knew we was here.'

'I see,' said Homily unhappily, and stared into the fire. Arrietty, looking down at her, saw Homily's hunched shoulders and the sudden empty look of her loosely hanging hands.

She turned again to her father. 'These ones are different,'

she assured him; 'they're not like Mabel and Sidney: they're tame, you see. I tamed Miss Menzies myself.'

'They're never tamed,' said Pod. 'One day they'll break out—one day, when you least expect it.'

'Not Miss Menzies,' protested Arrietty loyally.

Pod leaned forward. 'They don't mean it,' he explained, 'they just does it. It isn't their fault. In that they're pretty much like the rest of us: none of us means harm—we just does it.'

'You never did no harm, Pod,' protested Homily warmly.

'Not knowingly,' he conceded. He looked across at his daughter. 'Nor did Arrietty mean harm when she spoke to this Miss. But she did harm—she kept us deceived, like: she saw us planning away and not knowing—working away in our ignorance. And it didn't make her happy; now, did it, lass?'

'No,' Arrietty admitted, 'but all the same——'

'All right, all right,' Pod interrupted; he spoke quite quietly and still without reproach. 'I see how it was.' He sighed, and looked down at his hands.

'And she saw us, before we saw her,' Arrietty pointed out.

'I'd seen her,' said Pod.

'But you didn't know that she'd seen you.'

'You could have told me,' said Pod. He spoke so gently that the tears welled up in Arrietty's eyes. 'I'm sorry,' she gasped.

He did not speak for a moment and then he said: 'I'd have planned different, you see.'

'It wasn't Miss Menzies's fault that Mabel and Sidney took us.'

'I know that,' said Pod, 'but knowing different, I'd have planned different. We'd have been gone by then, and safely hidden away.'

'Gone? Where to?' exclaimed Homily.

'Plenty of places,' said Pod. 'Spiller knows of a mill—not far from here, is it, Spiller?—with one old human. Never sees a soul except for flour carters. And short-sighted at that. That's more the place for us, Homily.'

Homily was silent: she seemed to be thinking hard. Although her hands were gripped in her lap, her shoulders had straightened again.

'She loves us,' said Arrietty. 'Miss Menzies really loves us, Papa.'

He sighed. 'I don't see for why. But maybe she does. Like they do their pets—their cats and dogs and birds and such. Like your cousin Eggletina had that baby mouse, bringing it up by hand, teaching it tricks and such, and rubbing its coat up with velvet. But it ran away in the end, back to the other mice. And your Uncle Hendreary's second boy once had a cockroach. Fat as butter, it grew, in a cage he made out of a tea-strainer. But your mother never thought it was happy. Never a hungry moment that cockroach had, but that strainer was still a cage.'

'I see what you mean,' said Arrietty uncertainly.

'Spiller sees,' said Pod.

Arrietty glanced across at Spiller: the pointed face was still but the eyes were wild and bright. So wildly bright, they seemed to Arrietty, that she quickly looked away.

'You wouldn't see Spiller in a house like this,' said Pod, 'with everything all done for him and a lady human being watching through the window.'

'She doesn't,' exclaimed Arrietty hotly, 'she wouldn't!'

'As good as,' said Pod. 'And sooner or later the word gets around once humans know where you are—or where you're to be found at certain times of day, like. And there's always one they wants to tell, and that one tells another. And that Mabel and Sidney, finding us gone, where do you think they'll look? Here, of course. And I'll tell you for why: they'll think this lot stole us back.'

'But now we've got the fence,' Arrietty reminded him.

'Yes,' said Pod, 'they've wired us in nice now, like chickens in a hen-run. But what's even worse,' he went on, 'it's only a question of time before one of us gets caught out by a visitor. Day after day, they come in their hundreds, and all eyes, as you might say. No, Homily, it isn't taps and switches that count. Nor dressers and eiderdowns neither. You can pay too high for a bit of soft living, as we found out that time with Lupy. It's making your own way that counts and being easy in your mind, and I wouldn't never be easy here.'

There was silence for a moment. Homily touched the fire with a rusty nail which Spiller had used as a poker, and the slack flared up with a sudden brightness, lighting the walls and ceiling and the ring of thoughtful faces. 'Well, what are we going to do?' Homily asked at last.

'We're going,' said Pod.

'When?' asked Homily.

Pod turned to Spiller. 'Your boat's in ballast, ain't it?' Spiller nodded. 'Well, as soon as we've got it loaded.'

'Where are we going to?' asked Homily, in a tone of blank bewilderment. How many times, she wondered now, had she heard herself ask this question?

'To where we belong,' said Pod.

'Where's that?' asked Homily.

'You know as well as I do,' said Pod, 'some place that's quiet-like and secret, which humans couldn't find.'

'You mean that mill?'

'That's what I reckon,' said Pod. 'And I'm going by Spiller—no human ain't never seen *him*. We got timber, water, sacks, grain, and what food the old man eats. We got outdoors as well as in. And, say Spiller here keeps the boat in trim, there's nothing to stop us punting up here of an evening for a quick borrow round, like. Am I right, Spiller?'

Spiller nodded, and again there was silence. 'But you don't mean tonight, Pod?' Homily said at last: she suddenly looked very tired.

He shook his head. 'Nor tomorrow neither. We'll be some days loading, and better we take our time. If we play it careful and put this fire out, they've no call to think we're back. Weather's fair now and getting warmer. No need to rush it. I'll take a look at the site first and plan out the stuff we need. . . .' He rose stiffly and stretched his arms. 'What we need now', he said, stifling a yawn, 'is bed. And a good twelve hours of it.' Crossing the room, he took a plate from the shelf and slowly, methodically, he scooped up the ashes to cover the glowing slack.

As the room became darker, Homily said suddenly: 'Couldn't we try out the light?'

'The electric?' said Pod.

'Just once,' she pleaded.

'Don't see why not,' he said, and went to the switch by the door. Homily blew out the dips and, as almost explosively the room sprang to brightness, she covered her eyes with her hands. Arrietty, blinking hard, gazed interestedly about her: white and shadowless, the room stared starkly back. 'Oh, I don't like it,' she said.

'No more do I,' said Homily.

'But you see what I mean, Papa,' Arrietty pointed out as

though still seeking some acknowledgment, 'we could never have done this by ourselves!'

'And you'll see what *I* mean', he said quietly, 'when you get to be a little older.'

'What has age got to do with it?' she replied.

Pod's glance flickered across to Spiller and back again to Arrietty. Very thoughtful he looked, as though carefully choosing his words. 'Well, it's like this,' he said, 'if you can try to get my meaning: say, one day, you had a little place of your own. A little family maybe—supposing, like, you'd picked a good borrower. D'you think you'd go making up to humans? Never,' he said, and shook his head. 'And I'll tell you for why: you wouldn't want to do nothing to put that family in danger. Nor that borrower either. See what I mean?'

'Yes,' said Arrietty. She felt confused; and glad suddenly that, facing Pod, she stood with her back to Spiller.

'You won't always have us to look after you,' Pod went on, 'and I tell you now there's nothing never been gained by borrowers talking to humans. No matter how they seem, or what they say, or which things they promise you. It's never been worth the risk.'

Arrietty was silent.

'And Spiller agrees with me,' said Pod.

Homily, watching from her corner by the fireside, saw the tears well up in Arrietty's eyes and saw Arrietty swallow. 'That's enough for tonight, Pod,' she said quickly. 'Let's put out the light now and get ourselves to bed.'

'Let her just promise us,' said Pod, 'here under the electric, that she'll never do it again.'

'No need to promise, Pod—she understands. Like she did about the gas. Let's get to bed now.'

'I promise,' said Arrietty suddenly. She spoke quite loudly and clearly, and then she burst into tears.

'Now there's no need for that, Arrietty,' said Pod, going quickly towards her as Homily rose to her feet. 'No need to cry, lass, we was speaking for your own good, like.'

'I know,' gasped Arrietty from between her fingers.

'What's the matter, then? Tell us, Arrietty. Is it about the mill?'

'No, no,' she sobbed, 'I was thinking about Miss Menzies . . .'

'What about her?' said Homily.

'Now I've promised', gasped Arrietty, 'there'll be no one to tell her. She'll never know we escaped. She'll never know about Mabel and Sidney. She'll never know about the balloon. She'll never know we came back. She'll never know anything. All her life she'll be wondering. And lying awake in the nights . . .'

Above Arrietty's bowed head, Pod and Homily exchanged looks: neither seemed to know what to say.

'I didn't promise,' said Spiller suddenly, in his harshest, most corncrakey voice. They all turned and looked at him, and Arrietty took her hands from her face.

'You,' she exclaimed, staring. Spiller looked back at her, rubbing his ear with his sleeve. 'You mean', she went on, forgetting, in her amazement, her tear-stained cheeks and her usual shyness of Spiller, 'that *you*'d come back and tell her? You who've never been seen! You who're so crazy about cover! You who never even speak!'

He nodded curtly, looking straight back at her, his eyes alert and steady. Homily broke the silence. 'He'd do it for *you*, dear,' she said gently. And then, for some reason, she suddenly felt annoyed. 'But I've got to try and like him,' she

excused herself irritably. 'I've really got to try.' As she saw the disbelief on Arrietty's face change slowly to joyous surprise, she turned aside to Pod, and said brusquely: 'Put the light out now, for goodness' sake. And let's all get to bed.'

*   *   *

Stories never really end. They can go on and on— and on: it is just that at some point or another (as Mrs May once said to Kate) the teller ceases to tell them. With this last move towards a more hidden life, I come to the end of all I've really learned about borrowers. Without human witnesses there would be guess-work instead of evidence, and as far as I know (though you may have heard differently) no human has seen them again.

The story still goes on but it is your turn now to tell it. Much will continue to happen—things about which your guess will be just as true as mine. Arrietty will marry Spiller of course (we all know that), and they will have a fine adventurous life—far freer than that of her parents. Pod and Homily will be amazed at the distance 'these children' travel by boat and by the house they build among the tree-roots in the river bank—rooms upon rooms, with overhanging terraces; and their own secret well of spring water. Homily will grow anxious if they stay away too long, although messages will come downstream pretty regularly in the forms of skeleton leaves, rare grasses, or flower petals of certain colours—each with its own coded meaning. But as the years go by and Pod, growing older, climbs less easily and tires more quickly—she will become fonder and fonder of Spiller, who will care for them both to the end.

What I do know for certain is that Mr and Mrs Platter cut

their losses at Ballyhoggin and went to live near Mrs Platter's married daughter in London. Their last known address was 'Arundel', 105B Lower East Sheen Road, Surbiton.

Miss Menzies and Mr Pott stayed quietly where they were. When Mr Pott grew frailer, Miss Menzies decided to cook for him. As in everything she undertook, she became very good at it. Mr Pott was touched and grateful. As time went by he forgot his small, secret longings for steak-and-kidney pudding and grew quite to like her Bœuf à la Bourgignonne.

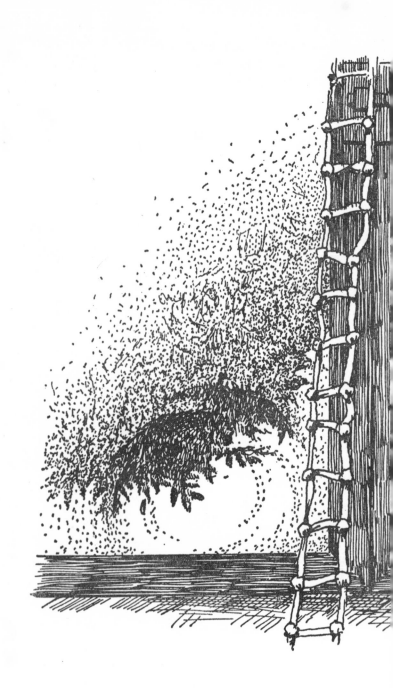